# PARISIAN NIGHTS

## ANONYMOUS

Carroll & Graf Publishers, Inc.
New York

First Carroll & Graf edition 1990

Carroll & Graf Publishers, Inc.
260 Fifth Avenue
New York, NY 10001

ISBN: 0-88184-561-2

Manufactured in the United States of America

# PART I

# I

A lady, young, fresh, extremely pretty and stylishly though quietly dressed, tripped daintily along a street in the neighbourhood of the Madeleine, in Paris, then disappeared into a respectable house, ran quickly up the stairs to the first floor and nervously pressed the button of the electric bell.

The tinkle had hardly ceased when the door was open by a neat maid who ushered the visitor into a handsome drawing-room in which were assembled sundry other ladies, all young and fashionably dressed, but all wearing the preoccupied air of persons about to have an interview with, say, their doctor or their solicitor.

Presently, as if awaiting the newcomer, the

mistress of the house appeared — tall, slender, exquisitely attired in black silk with a dainty head-dress of the style adopted by many English ladies of a certain age, possibly because of the undoubted air of distinction it confers. She smiled pleasantly at her young visitor as she shook hands with her; then with a murmured apology, she turned towards two of the other ladies and said: "Your friends have arrived and are awaiting you" — whereupon they rose and retired, smiling their thanks.

Turning again to her young visitor, she said affectionately: — "My dear, some one is waiting also to see you, a gentleman, one of my best friends. If you are willing to let him make your acquaintance, I shall be happy to introduce him to you."

This "good friend" was none other than myself! The house belonged to Madame de Saint-Edme, the most obliging of women and also the most tactful of her sex in the delicate mission of creating and establishing the most intimate of relations between persons of opposite sexes who desired to avail themselves of such services. To pretty women pressed for money or inconvenienced by their sexual appetites and desires, to mistresses "en titre" seeking to increase or supplement their alimony, and to married women who found their allowances insufficient or their husbands' powers not equal to the marital duties desired from them, Mme de Saint-Edme's discreet chambers offered the safest and pleasantest of opportunities for the acceptance incognito of financial or other assistance from gentlemen. Similarly she was ready to provide for gentlemen of amorous proclivities satisfactory opportunities of satisfying their carnal desires by the favours of impecunious ladies — thus avoiding on the one side a lengthy pursuit and on the other resistance before surrender.

Further again, those who loved to indulge in Lesbian practices found at her house a convenient *rendez-vous* where they could revel in the enjoyment of their sweet fantasy with the wished-for object of their desire, or (in her absence) they could there without difficulty come across girls who understood and shared their tastes, and who desired nothing better than to bestow or receive the lingual caresses so dear to tribades, lending themselves adorably to either of the two functions.

To old and trusted *habituées* (the younger fry being absolutely debarred unless there was not the slightest doubt as to their fidelity and discretion) she allowed the privilege of assisting at Lesbian-Priapus fêtes and representations to which were also invited such ladies as wished to be present and whose discretion was assured —

11

the lively feminine contingent knowing they had nothing to fear on such occasions where modesty was conspicuous by its absence.

She for who I was waiting was, according to Mme de Saint-Edme, a debutante in libertinage who had so far honoured her house once only with her presence. Said Mme de Saint-Edme to me:

— "I wanted you to be first to enjoy her, but you were unfortunately in the country when she finally plucked up her courage to visit me, having disappointed me twice previously. I wished very much that one of my good friends had been then on the spot, but alas, there were none! — And from fear of letting her slip away again, I introduced a casual visitor to her and she let him enjoy her! It was a rare good piece of luck for him, but now, at all events, we have caught our little bird."

Despite her cynically immoral principles, this excellent woman had the considerate delicacy to let her lady clients have a peep in secret at their respective proposed male companions, to decide whether they were pleased with them. Some fancied dark men, others fair — some admired beards, others preferred the simple moustache. Hot blooded and passionate woman sought for muscular strength coupled with distinction; cold blooded ones were more solicitous about the price they would receive for their favours. To these latter, the preliminary peep was only a formality of secondary importance.

It is no use to run counter to tastes — to clash with caprices. The ladies that were satisfied by their preliminary peep were forthwith conducted to the destined chamber and the introduction effected, a similar privilege and opportunity of inspecting his proposed lady companion having been accorded to the male client.

But as a rule these preliminaries were purely formal — thanks to the care that Mme de Saint-Edme took to bring together suitable partners, — thanks also to the skill with which she described to each in turn the charms of the other. And when the happy man was conducted to the allotted chamber (carefully furnished with every requirement a loving pair could desire) and introduced to the lady (who invariably made a pretence of doing needlework or reading when he was ushered in) Mme de Saint-Edme would disappear, the sequel not concerning her.

But when it was a case of a debutante she took care never to be far away! — for it was at the critical moment that the courage of the former failed them. "No! no! — not now! — not to-day! —" they would not unfrequently exclaim — and run out of the room. Then Mme de Saint-Edme would intercept them in the corridor, — and by means of her soothing caresses and persuasive words, she would induce them to stay. Then she would take them to another room and induce them to undress, — then whisper soothingly and encouragingly "Now dear, you are all right — I will go and bring him myself to you!" — and the episode would terminate with a bout of love made all the more delicious by the ardour imparted to the lover by a resistance that could only indicate that the girl he was about to enjoy was a novice in such matters!

But it must not be supposed that all the debutantes gave this trouble. After their second — and very often on their first visit — the majority of girls would not make any serious resistance to even the most audacious and libertine actions of their male companions. Very often indeed, instead of resorting to airs of startled innocence in order to stimulate their partner's lust, they would endeavour to attain to the same end by arraying themselves in the most provocative and decolleté costumes! Among her other virtues, Mme de Saint-Edme was able to give of the best advice as to the toilette to be adopted towards this end. It was not for nothing that she had been for years in one of the leading Parisian modistes establishments. In this situation, she had amassed much by pecuniary gifts from the clientele, both for her suggestions and still more for her services as a "broker-in-love", and the friendly relations she thus inspired invariably remained unimpaired.

On this occasion the lady whose favours had been retained for me had simply removed her hat, and I held mine respectfully in my hand while being introduced to her in the following words — "My dear, let me introduce to you the gentleman and friend regarding whom I have spoken to you!"

She turned to greet me, when — good Heaven! — I recognised a young cousin of mine! In our preliminary peeps we had seen each other but imperfectly, — her face had been in a great measure hidden by her matinée hat while it was no doubt my beard that made her fail to recognise me, for many years had passed since we had seen each other.

"Why? — it is you, Gilberte!"

Mme de Saint-Edme at once saw that she had unwittingly created an awkward situation — that she had "put her foot" into it! She stood dumbfounded! I begged her to leave us to ourselves.

The situation was piquant! This cousin was the "*petite cousin*" of authors, the "*petite cousine*" of youthful amorous indiscretions and yearnings which had not come to anything owing to her early marriage and the subsequent impossibility of rendez-vous, — and further, at such a time a woman does not lend herself to amorous adventures. I now found her grown into a beautiful

15

woman, — and under surroundings that (to me, at least) afforded an opportunity of reviving our youthful mutual passion and of carrying it to a satisfactory denouement.

She dropped her eyes in confusion! I took her hands gently in mine, and while assuring her that she could absolutely rely on my discretion I added that if she would like to go away she was at perfect liberty to do so and that I would never breathe a single word as to this meeting. But as my noble and chivalrously virtuous declaration did not produce any response, the mere man in me began to assert itself — and imperiously too! — as I contemplated the tumultuous heaving of her breasts under her dainty corsage and the betrayal by them of her emotions!

"Speak, Gilberte!" No answer. "Would you like me to go away?" Still silence.

I was puzzled to know what to do! Would it be advisable straightway to respect her and give up any attempt to induce her to accord to me favours she had evidently come prepared to accord to a stranger? Or should I treat her as if she was of easy morality, and without circumlocution address to her proposals that I would have made to any other woman I met under similar circumstances, and which I was justified in assuming would not be unwelcome to her? But women are so odd, their ideas of morality so extraordinary!

— and some who would in occasions submit themselves without hesitation to the grossest lubricity would on other occasions resent the least attempt at a liberty! At all events ladies that came to Mme de Saint-Edme's chambers could hardly expect to be considered as strictly virtuous — and Gilberte must rank herself with them! But our cousinly relationship — which at an ordinary society function would have assisted me — here was a positive handicap to both of us: I represented to Gilbert her family, her respectability, her past life, her girlish days!

I must confess that the memories of these latter were such as afforded to both of us a pretext for reviving the past in the present. In our youthful amusements we had not troubled to respect our mutual modesty! Stolen kisses, caresses of tongue against tongue, indiscreet ramblings of inquisitive hands under clothes, — all had brought us to the very threshold of the supreme pleasure. One day, when hidden in a barn with her, my hand had found its way to her little girlish cunny which it strove to excite by an active finger — while her little hands were amusing themselves with my prick as it stood rampant and stiff in her honour! But nothing else had transpired, and we had not met again, until now.

I reminded her of this, — she smiled, and little by little let fall her constraint, whether real or simulated.

"Don't speak of it!" she said — "we were sillies!"

"We certainly were, because we did not take advantage of our opportunities! But now that we have so unexpectedly met! . . ."

"Tell me, — didn't you know who I was when you came in?"

"Honestly, I did not."

"Well, suppose that you had made me out, would you then have come in?"

"It is possible that I might have considered it better in your interests to disappear, — but I should have done so with great regret, for you were looking so lovely! And you? — if you had recognised me?"

"I should have run away!"

"But why? Do you think I cannot appreciate your charms as well as any one else?"

"Oh! . . . But you and another man are two very different things! — you are a relative — and I had not come here for the purpose of meeting my family."

"I don't suppose you did!" I replied laughing. "But it is so easy for us to forget that we are relatives. I have only to think of you as a charming young lady I have for the first time met, — and you have only to allow me to make to this charming young lady declarations and proposals

18

to which I am sure she would like to listen much more than to remonstrances she might fear!"

"It seems to me so strange that I should be here at all with you! — I feel my presence here is so extraordinary — so upsetting!"

"Then, if we were to go on with our last meeting in the old barn, the sin (if any) would seem to you to be less grave and less piquant, — in fact almost allowable, as in marriage?"

"You're talking nonsense! . . . Of course not! . . . But to be seen by you here makes me feel as if everybody I know is also looking at me!"

"Then you don't care about doing this sort of thing before the world?"

Gilberte laughed frankly. I saw at once to what extent I should have adopted a false policy and how weak I should have been had I treated with an excess of respect a girl who, although my cousin, had of her own accord come to a house resorted to only by those who wished for a gratification of their sexual passions and desires! In fact, with any one else but her, I would before now have put myself in possession of charms which would have been surrendered to me kindly, — while had she been with any one else but me, she would not have concealed them from the eyes and no doubt the kisses of her happy companion!

"Well," I continued, "I don't know who you

19

are, — it is the first time I have seen you. Mme de Saint-Edme told me that she would introduce me to a charming girl who was visiting her for the first time, who proves to be even prettier than I could have anticipated, and who will, I trust, prove not less unkind than the others to whom Madame has introduced me and who have been good enough to amuse themselves with me here. May I ask what is your Christian name?"

"Gilberte," she replied laughing.

"Gilberte! What a pretty name! Well now, Gilberte, let me help you to take off your hat and cloak."

When I had hung these up, I passed my arm around her waist and kissed her on her mouth clasping her to me as I did so.

"You come here very seldom, I understand?" I said, — "I have not had the good fortune to meet you before."

"This is my first visit, Monsieur," she replied, entering into the spirit of the game.

"Really! But I think it cannot be the first time that you have left your husband in the lurch — for you look to me like a young married woman?"

"You are indiscreet, Monsieur!"

"Well — I won't press my curiosity any further! — at all events it is very sweet of you to allow others' to share with him in enjoying your charms."

Seating myself on a sofa, I drew her gently on to my knees, — I repeated my kisses on her mouth while my hand wandered inquisitively over her corsage. She laughed, — then exclaimed "Oh! Monsieur!" in the most natural way.

Then my hand descended a little, and pressed against and between her thighs over her dress. Her hand tried to push mine away! I yielded, — but only to pull up her skirts, in order to touch the bare flesh of what I had been feeling over her clothes! Gently I groped her calves, knees and thighs.

"Oh! . . . what are you doing, Monsieur?"

"Only trying to learn if you wear your garters above or below your knees."

"Above, always!"

"You have such sweet calves!" My hand climbed a little higher, — her skin was so soft and sweet!

"Oh! . . . oh! . . . you're tickling me! . . . No! . . . no! . . ."

"Why! . . . your drawers are closed in front! . . ."

"Ha! . . . ha! . . . oh! take away your hand! . . . you're tickling me! . . ."

"Oh! . . . now I've got to it! . . . Oh! . . . what a lot of hair you have! Ever so much more than you had in the barn!"

"What barn?"

21

"Ah! . . . pardon me! . . . I was forgetting!"

In spite of the re-appearance of the cousin under the lover, she did not stop or even hinder my delicious rovings among and over her most secret charms! This proceeding no doubt pleased her better than any sentimental modesty on my part, — it also pleased me better! Arranging her comfortably on my knees, my hand set to work to explore the delightfully rounded contours of her bottom—which I found plump, firm and springy.

"Madame," I said — "what lovely globes you have — real Maps of the World! . . . Very few girls have anything like your bottom, — so hard and so elastic!"

"What a comical name, Map of the World! Why?"

"Because there are there the two half-globes of the world. Do let me see them. Let me take off your corset! Oh! what a troublesome corset! Ah! now it is off! Oh! what lovely breasts! so nice and firm, as firm as your bottom!"

"Hush! you mustn't talk like that!"

"You are simply charming — delicious. I am charmed to make your acquaintance! No woman has ever inflamed me with desires to such an extent."

I seized her hand and placed it on the un-mistakable proof of the desires with which she had inspired me! She called me "*polisson*," which in the mouth of a woman is an encouragement to go still further, — and declared that I had not improved, I whom she had considered sentimental! I confessed to her that I was no longer so — that sentiment between men and women only tended to waste time and delay the pleasures of love.

"You then no longer are sentimental?" I asked.

"As you find me here you can see for yourself. Anyhow, all women sentimental or not, who talk about it, manage to finish in the same way, either sooner or later."

"You are making nice distinctions. You make me think you are a little student in love matters."

"Well, as to that, I fancy, I shall be still more so as soon as I escape out of your arms. You have a way of effecting this: I shall emerge from this truly accomplished."

This phrase spoken with a delicious smile, with that look that a woman knows how to use when she wishes to undress a man with her eyes and say to him, "Now come, let me see your," — this passage of words transported me with desire in indicating to me a horizon of endless pleasures with my lively cousin. I clasped her lovingly in my arms, exchanging, tongue-kisses with her, — then prayed her to undress herself.

I assisted her, seizing opportunity for deliciously touching her bare flesh, intoxicated by the sweet fragrance emanating from her undergarments which she had carefully selected — for every woman knows that the charms of her person are a treasure to be placed in a suitable frame to fairly show its beauty to the eyes privileged to view it.

Very soon she only had on her chemise! — in a jiffy I was in a similar costume: then after the necessary toilet we laid ourselves on the bed, closely clasped in each others arms, and abandoned ourselves to the sweet preliminaries to bliss.

"You will be discreet, eh?" said my cousin as she surrendered herself to me. To be so was of course as much to my interest as to hers.

Very soon she allowed herself to be invaded by symptoms of pleasure. Her lovely breasts began rapidly to heave, — her eyes half closed languorously. Was it real, or was she only pretending as part of her assumed role of a woman of pleasure? As she afterwards admitted that she had perfectly recognised me at the first and had allowed me to be introduced to her fully knowing the reason of my presence, it is quite possible that my handling and fingering of her naked body had the same rapid and sweet effect on her as when we indulged in our youthful escapades. As a matter of fact, it is the restless women who feel most sensitively the hand that caresses them. Gilberte, I recollect, used to go off at once, like a thorough-bred to the least pressure of the bit, — and now she had become a woman, she evidently had pre-served this precious quality. Anyhow, on my part, I was soon burning with the hottest lust. The girl I held in my arms inspired me at one and the same time with a craving for orgies such as one would indulge in with ladies of professed easy virtue, and the rage for such forbidden fruit gained additional piquancy from the fact that she was my cousin.

At my request she took off her chemise and displayed herself to me, naked, her lovely body relieved by the thicket of silky hairs that formed a triangular shadowing at the extremity of her rounded stomach, her nakedness being em-phasized by her shoes and stockings which she had kept on, by her garters which she adjusted above her knees when pulling her stockings tight. The little coquette knew well how a naked girl can heighten the effect of her nudity!

Then I felt and handled her all over, — I kissed and sucked her breasts. I thrust my nose under her arm-pits, diving amid the tufts of hair. There is nothing that imparts to one's desires so alluring a frenzy as the breathing of the "odor di femina" of the sweet body that has surrendered itself to you. My fingers nevertheless employed themselves in curling and twisting and playing with the mossy covering of her plump cunt, one of them caressing the delicious slit into which it soon forced its way, for the first time since our adventure in the barn. At that time, this cunny and slit were virgin! but my pleasure lost but little through this detail — for then her breasts were not so sweet a handful, her thighs were not so fat and round, her hips were not so full and plump, while the little hand that I had taught to play with my prick (oh! so timidly) was not so clever and soft. Her mouth then was not so skilled in the art of kissing, — while her chaste little ears would have closed themselves if I had whispered to them all that I was now softly murmuring to them while I gently agitated my finger over her clitoris.

"And what about this little pussy, this sweet little pussy? Does it love catching and eating mice? I will gladly give it mine!"

"It is a very big mouse, this one!"

"Girls like large pricks in their cunts! They are also charmed when a male tongue is applied. I want to apply mine to your cunt, — I want to do *minette* to you! You know what that is?"

She answered me simply with a smile. Promptly I placed my mouth on her closely clustering hairs (Gilberte was a lovely brunette) — I nibbled them with my lips, inhaling delightedly their fragrant perfume tempered with rice-powder and Eau de Lubin. Even as a young girl, this was her favourite scent, but then she did not apply it to this part of herself, no doubt in ignorance of the arts of provoking and spicing the audacious kisses that make the coldest girls faint with pleasure. But cold she never was, — and when my mouth settled itself on her cunt, when my tongue insinuated itself gently between its lips in search of the little spot in which a woman's sexual pleasure is concentrated, unmistakable symptoms indicating the most exquisite delight gave me to understand that she knew well how to taste this caress. One of her legs was thrown across my back and held me firmly to her, and I could feel the little heel of her dainty shoe dig into my ribs like a spur: the other foot she extended right down my front and against my prick and I could feel the soft leather that was rubbing against it.

Oh! what ecstacies! I could hear the broken breathings of my voluptuous companion, — I could feel her body quivering under the thrusts of my tongue, and the cheeks of her bottom wriggle in my hands as they gripped them. I felt her frenziedly press down my head between her thighs so as to let her taste every tongue-thrust. And I, twenty times was I on the point of flooding my cousin's shoe with the torrent of my discharge, — but I preferred to dispose of it otherwise. So at length, I released myself from her sweet clasp and placed myself again alongside of her on the sofa.

"Was it good? — did I do it properly?" I whispered to her.

"Very sweet indeed, you naughty man! It is very evident that you were not doing it for the first time!"

"And you? — is it the first time that you? . . ."

"You are horrid!"

"Ha! ha! Then you like having it done to you, eh!"

"All women do! But what do you think of one of my friends who declares she commits no infidelity towards her husband when she lets a man do her in this way?"

"I think I know her. Is she not a tall fair girl called Angela?"

"Yes. So you know her?"

"She comes here!"

"But how do you know that she is the one I mean?"

"Well! it is the same name, and she won't let a man do anything else to her but this."

"And have you then done it to her?"

"Yes! — I must admit it! — and it was well worth my while! But did she not also tell you that she confines her ministrations to her husband to this same one way?"

"Which way?"

I placed my finger softly on her mouth. Gilberte broke into laughter and asked if I had let Angela do me in the same way.

"Of course! — and what's more, I begged her to do it as she did not do any other way."

"Oh you men! — you dreadful men! Monsieur Henri!" (my Christian name). "I would not have believed you to be so . . . so . . ."

"So naughty? But in love many things that are naughty are also nice. But tell me — has no one ever asked you nicely to do it?"

"If I could say that no one had ever made such a request of me, I would not be able to say so for long — for I can read your intention in those eyes that are sparkling with lust!"

"Ah! — so I have missed also the virginity of your mouth! And so you have already committed this sweet sin! Was it in this house? Tell me all about it?"

"I don't remember!"

"Oh yes you do! — now do tell me, — whisper in my ear as if you were with your confessor!"

"You're a fine confessor."

"At all events not a cruel one! Listen:

Ma fille pour pénitence,
Et ron, ron, ron, petit patapon,
Ma fille, pour pénitence,

29

Nous recommencerons.

"Come, I'll give you a start! — you've done it once, twice, thrice, the first time out of curiosity, the second . . ."

"Oh! once will do! . . . I think I was mad that day! . . . A girl friend had invited me to supper with her and her lover, — and after dessert we all were a trifle squiffy! They told me all sorts of naughty stories, and they didn't mind what they did before me! In short, I watched them do all sorts of things till I was completely upset and excited beyond my self-control! . . . till unable to stand their teasing and challenges I let myself go in rivalry of my friend's libertinage and let her see me do with her lover all that she herself had just done with him!"

"And your friend was not jealous? And this is how you learnt this sweet little vice?"

"Alas! yes, — I must admit it!"

It is a well established fact that it is by their own sex and not by men that women are initiated into the most ingenious refinements of lust: and Casanova correctly recognised the fact when he maintained that a gallant who could manage to bring to one and the same rendezvous two girls hitherto enjoyed my him separately, would realise with the two together the most erotic of debauches. But as far as I was concerned, I was going to take advantage of what I had so happily found out, — and so continued to play my part as Gilberte's Father Confessor.

"Very good, my daughter!" I said to her. "And since then, how often?"

"I haven't done it since, Father," she replied laughing.

"My daughter, you must be nearly a saint! But nevertheless you must do penance!"

> Et pour pénitence
> Nous recommencerons, ron, ron,
> Nous recommencerons.

She resisted a little, saying that she was not worked up as on that occasion, that she didn't wish to do it again, that she had promised herself not to repeat the performance . . . But the example of her friend which I recalled to her soon overcame these feeble hesitations — coming as they did from her head and not from her inclination.

"Oh!" she exclaimed, as she bent down towards the object that stood rampant and stiff, burning to receive her caress. — "I don't think Angela would have waited till she was asked twice! — she loves doing it! Say!" she added with a malicious smile, "when we were in the old barn we didn't get as far as this, eh?"

Her soft hand guided my pego towards her lips and I felt it enter into her mouth, the moist warmth of which caused a delicious quiver of pleasure from my thighs to my loins. For a beginner she acquitted herself divinely: she took my prick well into her mouth, and with the recollection of her friend's methods in her mind, she set to work to give me the most intense pleasure in her power! Oh! my exquisite bliss! . . . my delirious sensations! Twenty times I was on the point of spending! . . . twenty times did I make her moderate her sweet suction so as to avoid spending, to postpone for the moment the ecstatic crisis! . . . twenty times did I ask myself in my rapturous transports whether I might let myself go! whether I might not expire deliciously in the mouth of the sweet girl whose fair head I could see as it rose and fell in cadence with the agitated movements of my body!

When a man is being thus blissfully ministered to by a woman who has a taste for this method — a taste that is more common than people believe, and which sometimes betrays its votaries when they are in the act of eating thick asparagus — and has reason to guess it, he can fairly let the sweet operation pursue its natural course and deposit his spermatic nectar on the pretty lips or in the dear mouth that has extracted it from him. But it is not less delicious to pour it, tripled in quantity by such a caress, into a cunt prepared by a similar caress and burning to receive it! And I shrewdly believe that while women may be willing on subsequent occasions to receive in their mouths the tribute of their lover's ardour, they are reluctant to do so on the first occasion on which they consent to effect this sweetest of ministrations!

Accordingly, placing my hand softly on her forehead, I reluctantly arrested the up and down movement of my cousin's head as she sucked my prick with a frenzy that seemed to indicate that she was fully sharing the pleasure she was giving me!

She looked at me in surprise, as if astonished at being stopped before the appearance of the unmistakable indication that her sweet duty had been accomplished! — the fact being that her friend (whose performance she had witnessed and was not following) never stopped her sucking until the "situation had been liquidated!" — as good Mme de Saint-Edme put it. And possibly on that memorable evening Gilberte also had . . .! Not having the skill of her Father Confessor, my interrogatories on this point had not been sufficiently direct and her confession remained complete!

So Gilberte, with a flushed and rosy face and moist lips, got up, and placing herself by me asked me if she had done it properly.

"Most charmingly, dearie, — quite as well as your friend!" I murmured as I kissed her on her mouth and passed my tongue over her lips all wet and humid! "Now darling, come! . . . on me, eh!"

Without a moment's delay she placed herself on top astride of me, — and quickly I shoved into her cunt my prick all moist with her kisses!

Suddenly, while lying on me thus transfixed and clasped in my arms, quivering with pleasure and jogging herself up and down in rhythm with my movements, she whispered, "But when you were . . . with my . . . friend . . . how . . . did you . . . do it . . . for she won't do . . . what we . . . are now doing . . .?"

"You must know! . . . a pretty woman . . . is . . . all cunt! . . ."

"You . . . dreadful man! . . . So . . . it was in her . . . mouth . . . always? . . ."

"Well! . . . Yes! . . . But you . . . are forcing . . . secrets . . . out of me."

"Then why . . . didn't you do so . . . with me? . . . I . . . was doing . . . the same thing . . . to . . . you? . . ."

"Are you . . . sorry . . . I didn't? . . ."

"No! . . . I only . . . wanted to know!"

"Well, because . . . I fancied . . . you didn't care . . . only . . . for this . . . like Angela!"

"That was very kind of you! . . . Well . . . one won't get . . . children . . . that way . . . that's something! . . ."

"So . . . next time . . . you wish me . . . to . . . spend . . . in your mouth . . . like . . . Angela does?"

She smiled, nodded her head slightly, — then closed her eyes voluptuously as if not to lose a single particle of the pleasure that was now thrilling through her whole person. For a moment I had an idea of resuming the sweet exercise we had just abandoned, — but the keenness of my present pleasure retained me at my delicious post beneath her! For the most exquisite of crises was approaching! Our tongues intertwined, our lips met, our movements accelerated! . . . oh! . . . now! . . . now! "Oh!"

Just at the critical moment, I took the precaution to swing Gilberte from the danger of presenting me with more cousins! I spent wildly outside her, my discharge shooting up into the air and falling like hot rain on her bottom and loins!

We had half-dressed ourselves again when we heard a knock at the door. It was Mme de Saint-Edme, who had come to see if we wanted anything. We asked her to bring us some refreshments. She seemed delighted and relieved to note from our deshabillé that not unpleasant sequel had followed her mistake in introducing us to each other.

In due course my cousin, now fully dressed and gloved, gave me a parting kiss through her veil, — and before leaving me arranged with me a further rendez-vous, — at which I promised myself (with a thrill of concupiscence) the pleasure of treating her as I did her friend Angela. I then called a carriage for her, a concluding attention that a woman appreciates after an amorous escapade.

"Well," said Mme de Saint-Edme to me after Gilberte had gone, "so you are satisfied! I was terribly afraid of scandal when I saw you knew that lady! Is she a relation of yours?"

"No. I used to know her when she was a young girl!"

"Oh! Well, I was very afraid of a scene!"

"Thanks to me, dear lady, there wasn't one!"

"I do thank you, — but some how I felt sure that you would arrange the matter without any scandal: another thing that reassured me was the air of distinction the lady had, — a woman of that caste hates a row. I feel the same also: do what you like, — amuse yourself as you may wish with the ladies, — all this concerns nobody else, and does harm to no one!"

"Rather the contrary," I rejoined.

"But do it in the proper way, — maintain appearances!"

36

"Pleasure coupled with discretion — that's my rule!"

"Oh! I'm not referring to you, — it's a pleasure to do anything for you! But all the same, when you asked me to leave the room, you looked a little afraid!"

"But now, you are reassured?"

"Oh! now she has once passed through your hands, she will be all right."

On the day arranged between Gilberte and myself, I attented at Mme de Saint-Edme's house. She escorted me to the chamber she had got ready for us, where she left me alone. I was the first at the rendez-vous, — and I must have waited some little time when she came in to tell me that my fair cousin had just arrived but that just at that moment a lady "habituée" had stopped her in the corridor and was expressing surprise at meeting her here.

"Why, Gilberte!" she had exclaimed — "I never thought of meeting you here! — you always used to say you dared not come! Have you come then to meet somebody?"

As Gilberte, surprised unpleasantly, hesitated — not knowing what to say, Mme de Saint-Edme came up and told her that her visitor had already arrived, — whereupon the other lady had remarked that it was a pity, but nevertheless continued her conversation.

This lady (I had very little doubt) was the blonde friend of Gilberte, Angela de Valençay, an adopted name, as I learnt later on, without my having done anything to pierce the veil of anonymity with which she (like the rest) strove to hide her visits for the purposes of satisfying and gratifying her secret passions.

"At all events, she does not seem to be jealous!" I asked Mme de Saint-Edme.

"Not in the least. She would not mind lending her lovers to her friends. But she objects strongly to any one being jealous of her. That seems fair enough."

Gilberte had not yet appeared.

"If she lets herself begin chattering with her friend, you may have to wait a long time," said Mme de Saint-Edme. "But it is all right — here they come, both of them. Ladies, you are being anxiously waited for!"

"Oh! no one's waiting for me!' exclaimed Mme de Valençay, — "all have made their arrangements for their fuckings and fun, for I notice the refreshments all over the place."

She indicated a table on which stood afternoon tea already laid out, which I had ordered in anticipation of Gilberte's arrival. I invited her to join us.

"But shan't I be in the way?" she replied. "Two turtle-doves like best to be alone! Very well — if I shall not be in the way, I will join you with pleasure, — only you must tell me when I am to disappear. You will respect my modesty, I am sure!"

But as she spoke she looked at me in a way that sufficiently indicated that her wishes were the very opposite of her words: her ardent glances seemed intended to recall to me past pleasures shared together and to invite me to the further joys she was evidently ready to give me. Dressed simply in a black costume, and carrying herself in a quiet manner but with an air of distinction, there was nothing about her to betray the lascivious desires that had brought her here, or the lecherous fashion in which she was ready to conduct herself — unless it was that peculiar glance that allowed one to detect, beneath the woman dressed, the naked woman, and behind perfect Society manners the intimate familiarity with the most daring libertinage.

While she was apologising to Gilberte for the liberty she was allowing herself to take, I had called for another plate and had dismissed her cab: for she had said that she hesitated to rejoin a cab that had been waiting at the door so long, — a feeling and accession of shame that a woman on an amorous escapade will well understand and which is often experienced when the time comes for her to quit the sweet seclusion in which she has been surrendering herself to her lust.

Then when the ladies had removed their hats and mantles we sat down at the table. Thus I found myself between the two pretty women, one a blonde, the other almost a brunette — a charming contrast! Each of them had been enjoyed by me separately — but this fact did not in the least diminish the power of their charms over me — and their joint presence, the sweet proximity of these two appetising feminine bodies to me aroused in my flesh the wildest lust which I hoped in turn to communicate to them.

The idea that each of them had been previously enjoyed by me made them both somewhat constrained at first, especially Gilberte, who seemed almost jealous: but very soon, under the soothing influence of "five o'clock tea" skilfully prepared, snatched kisses and licentious handlings, this slight constraint disappeared like dew under a morning sun. My mouth hotly attacked theirs alternately, — my tongue greedily sought theirs in turn, finding them only too ready to respond. Finally, when I was busily occupied with Gilberte, sucking her tongue, while my hands actively wandered all over her, unbuttoning her dress and stealing up her legs under her clothes till it reached the silken-haired centre of attraction which my finger then sought to inflame, I felt Mme de Valençay's hand pass over my trousers and attempt to drag into the air my torch of love, now fully alight and getting stiffer and stiffer in her fingers! Then away went all reserve! I begged them to undress or at all events to throw open their clothes so as to let me see, feel, handle and kiss more at my ease the two pairs of lovely breasts of which now I could only get a glimpse.

"But I say," exclaimed Mme de Valençay laughingly, "if you're going to ask your guest to undress herself, your invitation in place of being a simple one to lunch will be one including a dance!"

"When a lady is invited to dinner," I replied, "she naturally expects to stay and see the fun that is sure to follow."

"Ah! a play for three, eh?" she rejoined gaily, "but not arranged by the ballet-master of the Opera! Well, there's no reason why it should prove any the less entertaining, is there Gilberte?"

Gilberte smiled, half-pleased, half-vexed, — not from any sense of offended propriety but from a sort of feeling that as a comparative novice in amorous orgies she might have to play second fiddle to her friend! But her semi-hesitation only added a piquancy to her final surrender of herself, and did not hinder a woman of my cousin's disposition from letting herself go freely to learn fresh experiences in lust.

Mme de Valençay was already busy (in accordance with my request) to release from their confinement the two prisoners whom I had begged her to set at liberty. To effect this she had taken off her light blue silk stays, — and my lady readers will fully comprehend how the removal of a corset causes the dropping of petticoats unless held up by the hand: Mme de Valençay did not bother to do this, and so when the exciting rustling noise made by feminine garments being hurriedly taken off and thrown on a chair had ceased, she had on only a half-transparent chemise when she returned smiling to my side! Gilberte, after a little pressing, followed suit, and soon was similarly attired. As for me, I rapidly divested myself of all my clothes, — and Mme de Valençay's hand — Gilberte's also — was able to learn without hindrance the state in which I had been driven by the sight of the charms they were now exposing naked to me!

Then we set to work to play the fool! to commit a thousand erotic follies! We took chocolates from each others mouths: with my lips, I set to work to nibble one balanced on the nipple of one of their breasts, tickling her delightfully in so doing. Then I made a minute and close inspection of my companions' breasts, of the hairs under their armpits, also of what grew on their hills, light and golden on Mme de Valençay's, auburn and plentiful on Gilberte's. They both lent themselves to these games with a grace and freedom that was simply charming. At each fresh indecency that she found herself committing, Gilberte blushed shamefacedly, her bashful modesty being increased by the presence of a witness. Having kissed with ardour all the charms that I had been comparing, dividing my admiration and tribute equally between my fair companions, I proceeded to cover with kisses the two mossy hills of Venus they were exhibiting to my delighted eyes. Kneeling in turn before each one and between her legs, my mouth played lovingly with their curling hairs, every now and then touching with my tongue the sweetly hidden slit, and eliciting from them little shrieks of pleasure. Suddenly, under a libertine inspiration, I took from the table two chocolate creams, and having slipped them into each of their cunts to their great surprise, I announced my intention of eating them there, and proceeded to do so taking Gilberte first.

"Oh! what an ideal," she exclaimed, quivering and palpitating with pleasure as my tongue discovered the fondant between the lips of her cunt and having dislodged and rolled it over her clitoris!

"Oh! make haste! make haste!" cried Mme de Valençay, "mine's beginning to melt!"

And truly, when I planted my mouth between her thighs on the lovely slit that she impatiently presented to me, my tongue had really to hunt for her chocolate, to dive and burrow deeply in the charming cleft, only to find a trace or two and the aroma of the flavouring. Oh! how delicious her flesh tasted, thus sugared!

With such erotic pranks and antics our desires increased and grew stronger. Mme de Valençay, now quite wild with lust, took a candied cherry in its paper covering, and having removed the envelope she made me sit down — then kneeling before me she pulled up my shirt, seized my priapus with one hand, and with the other balanced the cherry on the cherry coloured gland which was rivalling its complexion. With smiles of delight she contemplated the result, — then suddenly, with sparkling eyes and heaving breasts, she moved her mouth forward and engulfed the cherry — and with it the head of my member, thus bestowing on it that most delicious of caresses which makes the happy recipient long to employ his mouth in a similar fashion and which impels the loving pair to satisfy their mutual cravings in a sweet *"soixante-neuf"*! Burning with this desire, I clutched hold of Gilberte who was busy kissing me and sucking my tongue, and was just going to propose to gamahuche her when she exclaimed: "Come it's my turn now,

Angela!"

Forthwith Mme de Valençay rose reluctantly, her lips moist, her face flushed. Gilberte immediately slipped into her place, and had already put my pintle (still wet with her friend's kisses) into her mouth when the latter cried out. "Why! you've forgotten the cherry!"

Quickly Gilberte, blushingly repaired this omission, and then I felt my prick again put into her mouth and sucked with ardour! Mme de Valençay had come back to her old place at my side, and while she finished eating the cherry she had taken, she watched with curiosity, whose pretty head was now bent down between my thighs. I slipped my arm round Mme de Valençay's waist, — our lips and tongues met in kisses into which I strove to put the burning pleasure that I was tasting from Gilberte! But I wanted something more! I wanted with my mouth to pass on to her exquisite sensations that were thrilling through me!

"Do let me do '*minette*' to you!" I murmured.

"All right," she replied, "but not here, as we now are! Let's go to the bed!"

This forced Gilberte to interrupt her ardent suction, — and when she had risen from between my thighs, I lovingly kissed her lips still fragrant with the scent of the fruit she had just eaten. And so we moved towards the bed. As we reached it, I begged the ladies to take off their chemises.

"No!" replied Mme de Valençay, "but this will be better still!"

Cognisant of Mme de Saint-Edme's forethought in matters erotic, she opened a drawer and took out two dressing-gowns made of the thinnest and most transparent material possible to image, one black and the other rose-tint.

"The black one will suit me as I am blonde," she said, — "don't look!"

She let her chemise slip down and replaced it by the dressing-gown, the transparency of which seemed to heighten the brilliant hue of her skin without in any way veiling the nakedness, but making it more piquant still! Moreover she did not fasten it in front, — but on the contrary she allowed it to float open on each side of her — thus displaying her lovely body naked from her stockings to the velvet ribbon round her throat! In this adorable costume, she placed herself in front of me and saluted me in military fashion.

"All in order, Monsieur!" she said — "see! I'm naked — yet I'm — not!"

My cousin slipped on the rose-tinted dressing-gown.

"I'm absolutely naked in this!" she exclaimed laughing!

"That is exactly as you ought to be!" I replied smiling.

Being then stretched out on the bed between my two pretty guardians whom I kissed and felt all over while their little hands contended for the control over my member, I was trying to decide which one of them I would choose in which to extinguish the fires of my concupiscence — when Angela who then was holding my prick tightly with her fingers, said:

"Who is to have this first?"

"Better draw for it!" I replied, "guess how many?" — and I took in my hand a lot of hairpins. Gilberte's guess was the nearest.

"Don't forget me, Gilberte!" said her friend, — "leave a little for me!"

But as I began to place myself between Gilberte's legs so as to put my prick into her cunt and fuck her, she appeared surprised, — then declared that she understood that she was to do what she had been doing to me on the sofa, viz, suck my prick!

"For you know," she explained, "Angela won't do anything else!"

"Oh! don't give me away like this, silly!" exclaimed her friend.

"Do you know that you are a charming and ravishing naughty little girl, just as she is?" I said, kissing her lovingly. "Well, do you also prefer . . .?"

Her response was to gently slip out from under

me and to lay me on my back in her place, — and as soon as she had got me properly extended on the bed, she, without loss of time, lowered her face towards the God Priapus. I felt her lips kiss the burning head, then her mouth envelop it, engulfing it deeply! Then I took up the thread of my caresses with Mme de Valençay; I drew her to me, kissed her lips, and let her tongue play on mine.

"Let me do *minette* to you," I murmured.

"Yes, dear."

Smiling lovingly at me, Mme de Valençay placed herself in position by straddling across my upturned face, arranging herself so that her cunt rested on my mouth, her face being turned towards Gilberte who had not stopped her sweet employment and who she watched at work intently. My tongue attacked her cunt eagerly, plunging deeply into it. I sucked her excited clitoris! — I licked passionately her warm and throbbing slit from end to end! Many times before this, had I enjoyed this privilege and pleasure, but always without the accompaniment of the spicy sucking that was doubling my transports and was impelling me to pass on to her the delirious fury that was agitating me!

Oh! the indescribable ecstasy! — to be sucked by one lovely woman while sucking another! Oh! the delightful postures of this doubled "*soixante-*

*neuf*" which permitted my lascivious fair friends to taste the most piquant voluptuousness equally with myself! But soon I felt that the torrent of my sperm would overcome my efforts to restrain it so as to prolong my present bliss!

"Gilberte! Gilberte!" I gasped brokenly, ceasing for the moment my sweet intentions to Mme de Valençay's cunt — "Gilberte! . . . I'm going to . . . spend . . . in your mouth . . .!"

I saw her head quickly nod a sanction which after all was perhaps superfluous after our recent meeting. My mouth returned to Mme de Valençay's cunt, my tongue resumed its voluptuous occupation with an ardour now unfettered by my efforts to retard my pleasure! Then came the ecstatic crisis! In my paroxysms of rapturous pleasure, my hands closed on my cousin's head, stopping the movements of her mouth! — I thrust my prick wildly down her throat! — my tongue madly darted deeply into Mme de Valençay's cunt! — . . . Oh! . . . Oh! . . . I spent! . . . I spent!! . . .

My boiling discharge shot in jets into Gilberte's mouth, making her retire in the middle of the eruption! Mme de Valençay, half fainting with pleasure, dropped limply on me! . . . We lay motionless till our energies revived. Then Gilberte wiped her mouth with her dressing-gown.

"I believe I've swallowed some of it!" she exclaimed laughing.

Mme de Valençay's head happened to be close to Gilberte at the moment when the latter drew back with filled mouth in the middle of my discharge, and she got the rest of it on her face, — which made her laughingly tell Gilberte that the latter had kept her promise to leave a little for her. Then she slipped off the bed and hurried off to the dressing-room, picking up her dressing-gown and holding above her waist as a woman does when she fears that her chemise may get compromising traces! Of course in this case there was no such fear, — but the result was to exhibit the most charming contours! Gilberte in turn went off also to wash off the traces of her recent occupation, for which purpose she did not require to use the bidet! I also imitated them, for my mouth, my lips, my moustache, all bore evidence of Mme de Valençay's warm feminine essence!

While I was thus occupied, Gilberte returned and lay down carelessly on the sofa. Mme de Valençay went to her, and placing her hand laughingly on her pretty calves began to amuse herself by running her fingers softly up and down Gilberte's legs. But when she got above the knee, Gilberte stopped her.

"Chut! . . . Not here! . . . Not before everybody!"

"It isn't before *everybody*!"

"Please don't trouble about me!" I said.

This little gust of passionate affection concluded for the time with a kiss from Angela to her friend, which clearly meant a great deal. There was no doubt about it! — my delicious companions were worshippers at the shrine of the Lesbian Venus! This revelation did not surprise me as far as Mme de Valençay was concerned, — to so voluptuous a woman nothing that was connected with sexual pleasures would be unknown to her, — but I never imagined that my naughty little cousin also had this fantasy! I was far from being displeased at this discovery, and I had the curiosity to ask since when had they mutually enjoyed each other. Then to my surprise, I learnt that it was Gilberte who had in the first instance seduced Angela! As girls they were great friends, — and one day, or rather night, an overflow of guests at a country house at which they were staying compelled their hostess to ask them to share the same bed. And oddly enough, it then came out that I must also have been a guest on that very occasion! Among my dancing partners was a certain Mlle B..., the fiancée of a happy mortal introduced to me as Monsieur R..., a Colonel in civil employ in the War Office. This girl had become Madame R..., and her husband

51

having obtained rapid promotion (as well may be imagined) was now one of the pillars of the Administration! As for her, after that valse with me, she had under an assumed name executed dances of quite a different nature, — and I had often had the pleasure of being her partner without either of us recognising the other!

"So after all, there is no reason why you should be so particular today, Gilberte!" I said, as I played gently with her bottom and her pretty white breasts. She only laughed and hid her face in her hands. We asked what was the cause of her merriment.

"Now, I come to think of it," she replied, "it must have been the very night on which you danced with Angela that she and I did! . . ."

"Of course in honour of myself and of all the partners that had pleased you!"

"But my dear," exclaimed Mme de Valençay, who continued to use this name, "you really are very indiscreet to tell Monsieur who I am! Fortunately he is your cousin instead of simply one of your lovers, and so the knowledge will not go any further. However, Monsieur, you must allow me to continue to be an entire stranger to you, should we ever happen to meet anywhere outside. Here I shall be delighted to continue on our old footing, and to place at your disposal myself and any talent I may have."

I promised, I swore to obey faithfully all her wishes, — and this little interlude did not divert the ardour that began to assert itself in our senses.

The thought that my cousin's friend, this lady whose naked charms I was enjoying, was really Mlle B... and now Mme R... the wife of a man high in office, — and that she came to this asylum of elegant immorality and discreet prostitution as a *habituée*, to yield herself to the most unrestrained demands of her lust, to the most erotic fantasies, — this thought did not tend to allay my concupiscence! Every sensation is heightened by contrast. A fair valley is doubly delicious after a painful toiling along burning rocks. The possession of a woman outwardly of rigid virtue seems to some preferable to having a beautiful courtesan! It is simply the idea of contrast that makes certain lovers dress their mistresses as nuns before rogering them! So with this woman, already so desirable while I thought she was simply a fast member of good Society (an opinion quite justified by her bold ways, her science in provocative arts, her freedom from prejudice as to the ways of enjoyment) what additional piquancy her favours acquired now that I knew that the lovely body she delighted to surrender to my licentious caresses was that of a well-bred and beautiful member of Society, respected in her circle, but who knew how to become debauched, naughty, almost as if she wished to make up for the time she was compelled, under the dictates of polite society, to behave as a "virtuous and godly matron!"

It was an agreeable sequel to my surprise when Gilberte, instead of manifesting by tears, refusals, etc. her dislike to seeing her position as a woman of respectability compromised in the eyes of some one that knew who she was, did not hesitate to be persuaded by the calls of her flesh and blood, — and resolving to see in me only a lover, lavished on me the pleasures of her person with an ardour and abandonment I could not have dreamt of!

So I renewed to both my fair friends my vows of discretion etc., adding that I swore on what I considered to be my most precious possession, viz, my prick, — which now was asserting itself boldly under the caresses of their delicate hands.

"Egoist!" they exclaimed, — "so what we have is not so precious according to your ideas!"

"What you girls have is to me the dearest of possessions and what I have to enable me to enjoy yours is to me the most precious."

"That is sweet of you! But I'm afraid that we are wasting good time!"

"And in a costume that in itself makes one wish to employ the time more sweetly!" added

54

Gilberte.

"Just listen to her!" exclaimed Mme de Valençay.

"Who loves me will follow me!" cried Gilberte, throwing herself on the bed.

And very shortly there raged between the three of us a storm of kisses, interspersed with exciting touchings and gropings and all the delicious preludes to a fresh bout of love! My hands wandered over two pairs of bubbies, two pairs of thighs: my mouth and my tongue played on theirs, deserting them at times in favour of two other mouths lower down and sweetly hairy — desertions which their charming owners did not seem to mind if I might judge by the sweet murmurs that came from the former as I licked and tickled the latter! Oh! if I only had two tongues so that I could gamahuche them both at the same time!

When at length I ceased and rose, I saw they both were on fire from the ardent way in which they kissed each other! Thereupon, I passed my arms round them, and drawing them close to me so that their lips and mine were touching I murmured "Oh! you two darlings! what a delicious and adorable pair of *gougnottes* you would make!"

A gentle cuff on my head told me that the word was not strange to my fair friends — but the smiles that their faces wore showed me that they were not displeased by my audacity.

"Won't you then do it before me?" I whispered — "do let me see you!"

"Oh! what a mad idea! . . . Well, what do you say, Gilberte?"

"Oh! I daren't! — I really couldn't! . . . see, we aren't by ourselves!"

"He won't look at you! . . . Come! . . . I want it! . . . I'll do it to you!"

Mme de Valençay slipped across me and gave my cousing several long clinging kisses, — then quickly placed her head between Gilberte's thighs, and soon the latter began to quiver under the action of the former's tongue! Leaning over my pretty cousin as she lay deliciously happy, I kissed her rosy lips, introducing my tongue between them as I revelled at the sight of these two naked lovely women surrendering themselves to their lesbian passions before me! Suddenly, Mme de Valençay stopped, raised herself, then flushing with delight, turned herself round and straddling across Gilberte, she placed herself on Gilberte, reversing herself. Her lovely backside sank down and hid her friend's face, — then settling herself down with a movement or two she placed over Gilberte's mouth the cunt that sought the lingual caresses which she recommenced on Gilberte's cunt! As for me, I delightedly contemplated the curtain of flesh which masked my cousin's face, the two plump and white buttocks which already had begun to agitate themselves in sweet tremors under the caress that had commenced. My hand passed lovingly over the rounded contours, — my lips deposited a hundred kisses on them, — and my tongue passing along the valley that separated them, travelled downwards till it nearly met Gilberte's, now in full operation on Mme de Valençay's cunt. But by this time it was not only a gentle tremor that agitated those charming globes of flesh, — it was a veritable storm of quivering heavings that indicated the approaching burst of her voluptuous discharge. I also, horribly excited, felt myself ready to spend, — but with a desperate effort I restrained, and eagerly watched my sweet pair of lesbians in the spasms of their spending! waiting impatiently for the finish of their ecstasy to beg one or the other of them to put out the fire that was blazing within me.

But no! They continued in their charming posture! . . . were they going to begin again? . . . oh! the naughty darlings! . . . they started afresh! I bent down towards Mme de Valençay, whose lips were playing on the lowest portion of the dark silky fleece on Gilberte's cunt. On seeing me she discontinued for a moment her charming employment.

"Are you going to do it again?" I asked eagerly.

"Well . . . yes! it's all your fault, you know! you've so excited us!"

"You naughty girls! O you're a pair of naughty, naughty girls!" I exclaimed — then kissed her luscious lips all moist and impregnated with Gilberte's spendings!

Before allowing her to resume her duties, I amused myself by playing with the hairs on my cousin's cunt. She began to do the same with one of her delicate hands!

"What lovely fur Gilberte has!" she murmured — "and pretty thighs!" she added as she passed her hands lovingly up and down over the satiny skin from the top of Gilberte's cream-coloured stockings right up to the sweet junction with her abdomen. I in turn did the same.

"Now, I begin to understand," I remarked "why one loves to get one's head between a girl's thighs even though one should be a girl!"

"Rather say because one is a girl!" she replied laughing, "for it is all that a girl can do unfortunately!"

"Now tell me," I continued seriously, "which gives a girl the intensest pleasure — to be sucked by a man or by a girl?"

My pretty companion laughed amusedly,

tickled at the idea of such a conversation being carried on in the silent presence of Gilberte's cunt. But at all event, she recognised that here was a chance to test the pleasing experiment.

"Gilberte!" she called out — "we are both going to do it to you, — tell us who does it best! you go on!" she whispered, pointing to Gilberte's cunt lying temptingly ready.

Her increasing agitation as betrayed by her voice clearly indicated that the fair judge was getting impatient and had recommenced her sweet ministrations to her friend's cunt! Quickly, I thrust my tongue into the charming slit so impatiently awaiting it, my salute being received with violent and rapturous transports! After a few moments, I made way for Mme de Valençay, who before long stopped for Gilberte's verdict. But the latter remained silent! — her tongue was too much occupied with Angela's cunt! and the fair owner, no longer able to restrain herself, stopped talking philosophy with me to give herself up to the imperative call of fast increasing pleasure. Thus the interesting experiment remained unsolved, ample opportunity being now available for some fair seeker after truth to test the efficiency of the male and the female tongue on her cunt! But I felt I could no longer remain an idle spectator of so voluptuous a combat! . . . I must cut in somehow!

"Would you like all you can get now?" I whispered in Mme de Valençay's ear.

"Yes! . . . yes! . . ." she answered, her tongue hard at work!

"You would? O you naughty thing! . . . You would like . . . *feuille de rose*?"

"Yes! . . . yes! . . . yes! . . .? she murmured with difficulty!

Promptly my tongue commenced to wander up and down between the firm yet elastic twin globes of her bottom, traversing the depths of the mysterious valley that separated her buttocks, thrusting, tickling, and working her into erotic fury. The naked bodies of the two girls plunged and twisted to the accompaniment of broken murmurs and inarticulate ejaculations! And I? Their lascivious transports sent me into a state of lustful excitement impossible to describe! — it was veritable torture! I could stand it no longer! — I must have something, some hole — a mouth, a cunt! I rushed behind Mme de Valençay as she lay astride across Gilberte's face, — I caught a glimpse of the cunt the latter was licking and sucking, — I slipped my rampant and furious prick between her nose, her lips and the grotto of love, — I drove her tongue away, — and rammed myself in! O the exquisite pleasure! — O the cunt, so soft, so deliciously warm and moist, so exquisitely lubricated by my cousin's minis-

trations! But I was soon forced to beat a retreat!
— it was contrary to the principles of my voluptuous partner to allow her cunt to be invaded in
this way, and in spite of my endeavours to the
contrary and the grip of her posteriors I had
effected in my desperation, she managed to dislodge me!

"O, you are very disobedient!" she exclaimed,
shaking her finger at me, "we must bring you to
order! O look at it! how angry it is, poor thing!"
— it was my raging prick that she was addressing
— "come! we'll soon calm you, Sir! Lie down!"
she added to me.

I released Gilberte, whose head had been imprisoned between my legs.

"You were in a funny position!' Mme de
Valençay said to her.

"You at all events cannot say that he didn't
have you, dear! At all events I could see! He went
into you up to your hair! O yes, you were
properly had that time, my love!

"As a matter of fact, you ought to have kept
him out!"

But by now, I was on my back. Mme de
Valençay, after some tender kisses, directed her
mouth to where a different function was eagerly
awaiting her. "After the cunt of the girl-cousin,
naturally comes the turn of the male-cousin's
prick!" she said, laughingly. I suggested to

Gilberte that she should let me suck her, and although she had already spent plentifully with her friend, she was none the less ready to commence anew! "Gladly! gladly!" she exclaimed, as she slipped across my face and adjusted her cunt so as to rest on my mouth!

I plunged my tongue wildly into it, though I was almost swooning with ecstatic rapture as Mme de Valençay devoted herself to my prick — kissing, sucking and tickling the gland with the tip of her warm tongue and her burning mouth, then allaying the poignant sensations thus excited by ardent and passionate suction. Then she would remain passive, retaining her prick in my mouth and letting me work it up and down deliciously between her lips! and when I stopped, she would resume the entrancing motion! It was a taste of Paradise that I would gladly have prolonged indefinitely! But this was impossible! I simply couldn't contain myself any more! My tongue redoubled its activity on Gilberte's clitoris! — my hands clenched Mme de Valençay's head! — between her delicious lips my prick worked itself faster . . . faster! . . . with a frenzied upward heave, I shoved it into her throat! — I surrendered myself wildly to my pleasure! . . . then spent . . . spent . . . spent . . . nearly swooning as I shot my three burning discharges into her mouth!

Without the least flinching, Mme de Valençay received and retained in her mouth this unceremonious homage to her charms, and also held as a prisoner the object that had caused the deluge, till its last spasm, — while Gilberte (who had spent equally deliciously on me) fell breathless and panting on me with a gasp of pleasure, — and thus we rested for some instants in rapturous oblivion.

\* \* \* \*

"What's the time?" asked Mme de Valençay, who had slipped on her chemise again and was engaged before the mirror with a powder puff. "Six o'clock".

"Heavens! And I have to dine out to-night! I shall hardly have time to get back and dress! My husband will be cross!"

"The same with me!" exclaimed Gilberte. "My husband will scold me!"

Quickly and hurriedly, the two ladies picked out their belongings from the mass of garments lying all over the room, — and soon put on their drawers (the most useless things where love is concerned) corsets, skirts, etc., and very soon were fully attired and ready to appear in public. I called carriages.

Just then Mme de Saint-Edme asked for a word

with Gilberte and whispered something to her.

"Not this afternoon! — I've no time" she replied.

"Only tell me if you would be willing and when."

"I would like it, — but I'll write."

Mme de Valençay caught her arm and asked what it was all about. Gilberte whispered something. I in turn asked for information, but the two ladies went off in fits of laughter.

Later on, I learnt that what had been asked of her and what she had accepted was to be introduced to a young and pretty actress who was well-known as a high-priestess of Lesbians, and who had desired to make my cousin's acquaintance and to cultivate her in the charming intimacy necessary to the cult. I venture to say that she will not be disappointed.

## II

"Well? And your loves? Have you brought your last conquest to a successful termination?"

The person who was thus questioning me was Madame de Liancourt, who I was about to accompany in her carriage at the close of a Charity Ball given at the Hotel C.

"What new conquest?" I asked.

"You know! The lady with whom you were seen in the Bois the other day! It was most imprudent on your part to thus compromise her! Now, was she not the wife of Maitre B., the lawyer?"

"What? Did you really see us? Do you know her? I assure you . . ."

"My dear man, you are defending yourself

very badly! But otherwise, my compliments to you! She really is very nice! And has she been . . . kind? She has the air of being a trifle too unsophisticated for you, but she is in excellent hands and will soon learn . . . eh? Tell me, have you already educated her to humour your . . . caprices?"

"Dear Madame! I assure you . . ."

"Come, come, — you needn't tell me this, me, your old pupil! You know I won't be jealous!"

"A pupil who has graduated with honour to her teacher and now possibly exceeds him!"

"Be polite, if you please! You men are really too awful! You teach a poor innocent girl all sorts of naughty things, and then you reproach her if she should put your lessons into practice!

"I reproach you? — on the contrary! I prefer you as you now are, so knowing, — so charmingly naughty!"

"Then tell me."

"Here comes your carriage! Haven't you changed your coachman?"

"Yes and no! Baptiste drives when I go out in domestic state in the company of my lord and master, my husband. But when I go by myself, I drop the family coachman and the family state and take a hired carriage. It is better in case of any . . . adventures, — for then I have nobody's indiscretions to fear! Baptiste for instance, knows you."

"Without knowing my successors!"

"You rude man! Come, open the carriage door for me!"

"May I not have the honour of accompanying you?"

"Oh, yes! I know what you mean! You don't deserve to be allowed! But you must behave properly! Tell the man to drive to Rue de Suresnes."

Since the termination of my liaison with Madame de Liancourt, a liaison which terminated without any rupture or unpleasantness, she (so she told me) had been leading a life without restraint and unfettered by any ties. She amused herself by studies in the physiology of Love, selecting her subjects for comparison how and where she pleased. Further, we had agreed to confide to each other the result of our various amatory adventures, and we did not interdict ourselves from renewing our former intimate relations if we so desired — if our electric currents should attract us to each other and if their tension should become such as to make the contact of our naked bodies bring about a "discharge" (truly, a scientific word, but one most appropriate for the occasion)!

This evening, we were in such a condition. Speaking for myself, the act of dancing, the sight of bare shoulders and breasts emerging from their lace surroundings as if to challenge men to consider whether what was hidden was likely to correspond with what was being shewn, all this had greatly excited me; and it did not make me any the calmer to be seated beside a lovely woman of about thirty, luscious and voluptuous to the degree at which a touch of maturity adds such spice to the charm of youth!

As for tell-tale eyes (which seemed to say "Do you remember?" and "Shall we re-commence?"), the gentle friction of her knees against mine as the carriage swayed, and a thousand other signs, showed me clearly that she was quite willing to satisfy with me the warm desire, the longing for a man which a hot-blooded woman feels after inhaling the masculine odour emanating from her dancing partners and after having abandoned herself to their more or less lascivious embrace. We could not but concentrate our ardent desires one for the other, — she, with all the burning longings of an erotically excited woman; I, with all the lustful ideas which riot through the brain of a man as he looks at pretty women and mentally undressing them imagines their appearance without clothes!

It was not therefore very surprising that before we had got half way to our destination, I threw my arm round Mme de Liancourt's waist, brought my face against hers, and set to work to kiss her on her mouth and with my tongue to seek hers. My disengaged hand slipped up under the frilly flounces of her ball-dress, crept along over her silk clad legs and over her garters, and little by little reached her drawers and found the opening — through which it passed and commenced to touch and play with the close clustering and mossy forest of silky curly hairs.

"Wretch!" gasped my companion, as she abandoned herself to the voluptuous sensations that my finger was communicating to her as it sought to bury itself in the warm moist slit! In kindly reciprocation, her white-gloved hand travelled over my trousers, till it found the unmistakable proof of my excited condition! Quickly sundry buttons yielded, — and then I felt against my sensitive skin the touch of dainty gloved fingers which promptly began their delicious manoeuvres, returning service for service, pleasure for pleasure!

Not a word passed! — only the sound of sighs, breathings, gaspings, as fingers and tongues busied themselves in their salacious duties! Oh, why is man not physically able (as a woman is) to sacrifice to Venus over and over again with hardly a pause, as women can? — Why must there as a rule be a break between one sacrifice and the next? With what delight would I have surrendered myself to the exquisitely maddening sensations communicated to my rampant prick by those gloved fingers and their subtle compression, even at the risk of ruining those white kid-gloves! But as I looked and hoped for a more completely satisfactory gratification of my lust before long, I managed to retain my burning ardour and keep it in reserve! More fortunate than me, Mme de Liancourt, whose soft smooth thighs kept squeezing my hand, let herself go! — gasping, panting, quivering, she clung to me, spasmodically agitating her heaving hips and bottom — then inundated my hand with the creamy dew of her ecstatic discharge!

Just then the carriage stopped. Hastily we adjusted our dress, and after sending the carriage away, we entered the house in which Mme de Liancourt's suite was located. A dim light had been left burning for her. As she passed the concierge's den she gave her name as Mme Germain, telling me after we had passed inside that this was the name by which she was known here.

The suite was on the first floor. Mme de Liancourt unlocked the door herself and ushered me into a handsomely furnished vestibule in which a rose-shaded lamp shed a soft light quite sufficient to illuminate the place. She remarked that she had done the furnishing, and that besides this there were a few more rooms.

"Here's the Temple!" she exclaimed, leading me into the bedroom, the best room of the suite. In it was a bed, large and low with thick curtains, a veritable theatre of Love! In one corner was one of those long and low easy chairs which accommodate so delightfully the form of a woman, especially when she is surrendering herself to furtive fondling and groping under her clothes! Numerous cushions were scattered all over the place; in another corner was a dainty stove; against one wall stood a full length mirror. A smaller room opening into the bedroom had been furnished as a dressing and bathroom; here one saw displayed and ready for use the whole of a woman's mysterious toilet equipage, low divans, bidet, douche, basins, jars of essences, bottles of scent; a third room also communicating with the bedroom served as a boudoir, but for the moment fulfilled the office of a supper room, as the table had been laid with a cold supper for two persons. Thick close carpets covered the whole of the floors, and each room was fitted after the convenient English fashion with gas heating and lighting apparatus, thus enabling the occupant to practically dispense with servants.

"Does your maid Justine attend on you here?"

"No, only the concierge's wife and her sister."

"But what do they think when they see you here?"

71

Madame de Liancourt smiled with a significant glance from her eyes and a gesture that plainly said that the presence of a gentleman would not occasion any surprise!

"Then they must have queer ideas about you?"

"My dear man, I have made the position quite simple and easy by not attempting to hide anything, but to pass as a *cocotte*. You see this cuts short all suppositions!"

Undoubtedly she had freed herself from traditions since I last had the honour of being entertained in her arms; and her candid admissions constituted in her quite a new attraction for me!

"Then this evening you are going to be my little cocotte!" I replied as I amorously kissed her mouth. She nodded, with a smile.

Then I proceeded to utilize with her to its best advantage her luxuriously equipped installation. I began by taking off her shoes, — and under the pretence that her high laced uppers rendered it necessary, I lifted the frilly flounces of her ball-dress and petticoats till the bewitching sight of a pretty woman's dainty underclothing was displayed to me, — the neatly shod tiny feet, the delicately rounded silk covered calves, the tempting garters above her knees, the strip of naked flesh just above them, her semi-transparent drawers with their frills, — all framed by the surrounding waves of her petticoats!

"What are you about? . . . come, do take off my shoes!"

But in spite of protests, I managed to deposit sundry hot kisses on the tempting bare flesh just above the garters; then in reluctant obedience I took off her shoes and helped her out of her ball-dress, — but not without permitting myself sundry libertine and wanton touches! How delicious it is to feel a girl's naked flesh under its gauzy covering, to pass one's hands over her back and loins, her lips and haunches, her bottom, when protected only by a thin chemise! — then turning one's attention to her front, to draw the light folds tightly round her so as to reveal her shapely round belly and thighs, to press the light material well in between her legs! O what delicious preliminaries! — and what riotous desires they kindle! And how girls always pretend to try and prevent the taking of such liberties, pleading shame as an incentive to induce the tickling which invariably results and which draws from them the inflaming little screams and wriggles they know so well how to give! My pretty companion did not disappoint me in this respect!

"Wait, wait!" she ejaculated as she freed herself from my audacious hands and ran towards the dressing-room, pausing at the door to say softly but significantly "I have danced a lot to-

73

night, and . . . I have not forgotten your . . . caprices!"

Could one be paid a more delicate attention or be given a more discreet invitation? Promptly I undressed myself, — then when Mme de Liancourt had quitted the dressing-room, I passed in, and presently I joined her on the bed on which she had laid herself.

"Let us stay as we are on the top and not under the sheets!" she suggested, — "it is warm."

"By all means, — and we can also see each other better!"

"You are just the same, — or rather worse than ever! You have already seen me all over, — you know every bit of me!"

"Yes, — but a man can't see too much of a pretty girl."

"You're very complimentary today! Well, if you must . . ."

She had on only a light dressing-gown, and nothing under it! not even a chemise! One by one, I undid the fastenings in front, and soon there was nothing to hide her naked beauty from her garters to her neck, round which she had retained a loop of velvet. Her white satin-like skin lay open to my sight interrupted only by the tawny gold patch that covered the lowest extremity of her belly with its clustering curls.

"You have grown a little fatter, my love," I

remarked as my hands passed over her naked flesh!

"Too much so?" she asked regarding herself.

"Oh no, — you're just perfect, just delicious!"

"And what about you? . . . The same as before?" With her soft hand she began to feel me, and little by little she approached the organ she had already so deliciously honoured during the drive, — then gently took hold of it!

"How stiff it is!" she said softly — "how it swells! — it seems quite pleased to meet its old friend! Eh? . . . You're very pleased, old chap, aren't you . . . eh? . . . eh? . . ." (she spoke as if to her pet dog). And you've seen cunts of every shade of hair since you last saw mine."

"As to hairs, yes," I replied, — "but nothing so adorable as this!" — (my readers can guess where my fingers now were!) What a lot you've got!"

"More than Madame Beaupré?"

"I haven't yet seen hers!"

"Come, come, what nonsense! Haven't you then even touched it?"

"Hers couldn't possibly be more lovely than yours!"

After many a burning kiss, many a thrilling tongueing, my mouth in its turn visited and explored all that my eyes had been feasting on, — my hands meanwhile playing with her neck, arms, shoulders, haunches, and then her saucy breasts — the nipples of which I playfully bit gently as I watched the lovely owner as she lay pleased and smiling. Then going a little lower, I pressed my lips through her hairs with the intention of working my way along her tender slit, with the result that my tongue was soon inside her cunt! Madame de Liancourt no longer smiled, she was now too much absorbed in the sensations of the moment — as was conclusively evident by her broken breathing and the wriggling movements of her loins, haunches, hips and bottom!

"Together! . . . both together!" she presently murmured, — then disengaged herself for a moment to pull back a curtain and reveal a large mirror in which one could see everything that passed on the bed!

"Isn't it shocking?" she laughed.

Then without further delay I placed myself on my back, my head between her legs, our bodies forming that delightful posture known as *soixante-neuf* . . . Reflected faithfully in the mirror, I could see the back of Mme de Liancourt, the adorable curves of her loins, her superb hips and haunches, the magnificent globes of her bottom — between which was visible my head framed by her plump round thighs, — while my thighs in turn flanked my voluptuous companion's bent down head, of which I could only see a few on the curls of her neck!

O what pleasures we tasted! what ecstatic quiverings thrilled through our bodies as our mouths emulated each other in their efforts to communicate to each other the most poignant and rapturous bliss! Mme de Liancourt devoted herself divinely to her sweet function! Although her mouth was small, she succeeded in making it large enough to get into it nearly the whole of my swollen and rampant prick, her fingers supplementing her lips as regards the portion left outside and making me feel exactly as if the whole of my organ was buried inside her mouth! On my side, my tongue (admittedly agile and clever by every woman who had allowed herself the experience) excelled itself in its efforts to drive Mme de Liancourt into indescribable ecstasy, ecstasy shared also by me, — for nothing can be more heavenly to the man than to feel the rapturous thrillings of pleasure as they vibrate through the woman to whom he is endeavouring to impart the most exquisite pleasure she is capable of tasting, and who is ready to forgive the immorality of the act so long as she is maintained in a heaven of blissfulness!

Having thoroughly teased, worried and tickled her clitoris with my tongue and excited it by tender nibbles of my teeth, I attacked the quivering lips of Mme de Liancourt's cunt, thrusting my tongue deeply between them and arousing in her a hitherto unfelt depth of pleasure, so keen and so voluptuous as to cause such violent agitation of her hips and the globes of her bottom, that although I was gripping the latter with my hands, I could scarcely restrain their plunging movements sufficiently to maintain my mouth on the dear object of its worship!

Finally we disengaged ourselves, and adopting the ordinary position I extended myself on the bosom of my voluptuous companion; she clasped me closely to her with her lovely arms, and in silence we united the parts of ourselves that our lips and our tongues now finding themselves together again sought mutual pardon for the lascivious caprice which had temporarily separated them! Oh! how delicious is the passage into a grotto that one has been kissing and sucking till the sweet interior has lubricated itself by successive spendings! — The heavenly up-and-down joggings are so delightfully facilitated, the pleasure becomes doubly sweet owing to the more intimate contact and union of sexual parts, while the girl now provoked into the highest pitch of erotic desire, quivering with unsatisfied lust and deliriously enjoying her position under her lover and the clasp of his arms, abandons herself ecstatically to the sensations of the moment in furious unison with him!

Presently, I saw Mme de Liancourt's eyes turn

upwards and half close as the first spasms of pleasure began to thrill through her.

"Gently! . . . gently! . . ." she gasped! . . . "Oh! . . . it's just heavenly! . . . gently darling! . . . oh! . . . oh! . . . wait! . . . wait! . . . I'm . . . just coming! . . . coming! . . . oh! . . . oh! . . ."

Our tumultuous plungings and heavings quickened frenziedly, then ceased in a storm of kisses!

\* \* \* \*

"O darling, what a deluge! I'm absolutely full of it!" And she rushed off to wash and purify herself.

After a visit in my turn to the lavatory, we were ready for supper: pâté de foie gras and old Sauterne are most excellent auxilliaries to Venus!

Mme de Liancourt had placed herself at the table with only a dressing-gown on. This did not remain fastened for long, — and then the spectacle of her naked charms and the sensations excited mutually by our inquistive and wandering hands quickly put us in train for more erotic scenes, which soon began to be reflected in the mirror.

"Tell me," said Mme de Liancourt, "have you ever done this with Mme de B."

"No."

"I can hardly believe you! Then for this particular caprice of yours you have come to your old pupil, your present one not yet being educated up to it! But no doubt you will before long gently break her to it, — just as if you were newly married husband and wife! I should like to see you at it! You might do much worse than to let me have her for a time to polish and finish her in these matters!"

"You're very kind! Only you would inspire her with desire for girls, not for men. You know you thus seduce all your girl friends in this particular way!"

"Come, come, — don't you speak evil of this fancy of mine, you of all people! — for except for it, you would never have met me! But don't you know that a woman can and does love to . . . amuse . . . herself with women as well as with men? I can, for instance!"

"Yes! that may be! — but there aren't many like you! Most girls go after either girls or men. You are essentially a woman of pleasure, devoted to pleasure, loving pleasure for the sake of pleasure, — ready to taste it in any form, with complete indifference to the sex of the person that is communicating pleasure to you!"

"I am not worse than you, my friend!"

"I'm not reproaching you! I'm simply stating a fact, which explains why we understand each other so splendidly! You have learnt how men can induce pleasure and how women can impart it, — and so you go from sex to sex audaciously experimenting, without being able to decide which you like the best!"

"I'm exactly like you in this respect, my friend!"

"Yes! but with this one important difference, — the feminine sex satisfies my exigencies and my curiosity and generally in every direction in which I may be tempted to pursue my researches!"

"Prettily spoken, my friend! — Still, had I your present sweetheart as a pupil, I would soon inculcate in her quite as excellent principles only more in accord with my tastes; I would impress her with myself as an example and also to keep her from concentrating herself on any one person, be it male or female! More over, unless I am deceived by the look of her eyes, she possesses the right temperament for my teaching; and I fancy it would not be long before your little innocent friend is ready and willing to lend herself to all sorts of salacious variations of carnal love, — and who knows? — may become the mistress both of yourself and of myself!"

Mme de Liancourt laughed merrily, then continued, — "But I won't ask for so much! I would like just to give her one lesson for your special benefit, — and I would even allow you to listen behind the door, so that you can judge for yourself whether I overstep the bounds of what a girl ought really to know!"

I fell in with her fantasy and I agreed to her suggestion. In my secret heart, the idea of having a woman as my rival in the affections of another woman was to me exceedingly piquant, — and I gladly left her to carry out her caprice.

*     *     *     *

Mme de Liancourt accompanied me one day when I had arranged to meet Martha; and as soon as we discovered the latter she went forward by herself to meet her as from me, while I slipped off to her chambers. Mme de Liancourt told Martha that the latter's husband was suspicious, and was endeavouring to have a watch kept on her. — And this was why I had not come to the rendezvous, — that I had asked her to come instead to explain and to bring her to where I was awaiting her. After a little hesitation, Martha consented to accompany her to the Rue de Suresnes.

Presently (hidden in the small boudoir) I saw them come in and pass into the bedroom.

"You're quite safe here! You're in my own rooms! Here you can bill and coo as much as you please with your lover!"

Martha coloured to the tips of her little ears.

"But, Madame, Monsieur R. isn't my lover! We have never . . ."

"Really? My child, you have done well to tell me this, — you need fear no indiscretion on my part, for I also have a lover! The danger you were running has made me take an interest in you, and this is why I gladly brought you here at the request of Monsieur R... Really it was almost heroic of me to do so, for there are not many women who would go out of their way to bring to a mutual male friend another woman younger and prettier than herself! But it is so, dear, for you are certainly prettier than me!"

She kissed Martha. Then she invited her to take off her wraps and to make herself at home. But when she observed that Martha remained fully dressed with the exception of her mantle, she said to her.

"Don't be afraid, dear! do make yourself at home and do as I do! You mustn't remain as you are and receive your lover so, — for men like to see their sweethearts in some déshabillé when they come to visit them, — besides this, I have to change my dress for my evening's engagements. It will be pleasant to take advantage of this and see how some of my dresses will look on you, — an excellent idea — for should any one have followed us here and finds us so engaged, it will completely throw them off the scent!"

I admired the cleverness of the argument!

Mme de Liancourt rapidly divested herself of her dress, corset, and petticoats till she had on her chemise only; then she proceeded to reduce Martha to a similar condition of undress, in spite of the latter's hesitation especially as to removing her corset, as she alleged that she should keep this on if she was to try on any dresses! This Mme de Liancourt would not agree to!

"You wear very pretty under-clothing, dear! — no doubt you study his tastes in such details?"

This was a good guess, — for Martha had put on the corset we had bought together, also the lace petticoats and the delicately trimmed chemise. How delicate is the female instinct in the matter of attracting the male amorous desires!

"I do not know whether my dress will fit you, dear," continued Mme de Liancourt. "I think I am bigger than you are in the bust!"

Under this pretext she threw open her chemise and exhibited her breasts, which she set to work to compare with those of Martha, after having first unfastened and opened the latter's chemise.

"What deliciously white and firm little bubbies you have, dear! I expect you have often been complimented on them! A very fortunate man is your lover, — of course I don't mean your husband, — for if the latter saw you thus, I suppose he would trop to spoil these little darlings, where as your lover would know how to show his appreciation of them by his caresses."

"Suppose he should suddenly turn up and catch us as we are!"

"I should rush off into any corner that I could!" replied Mme de Liancourt with a smile she endeavoured vainly to repress! She added:

"But at a ball we women show quite as much of ourselves as you and I are now doing! I, at all events, have my dresses cut low enough to let my nipples be seen! Besides, it is only a woman with a bad figure that objects to be found naked or practically so! I'm not one of that lot! — see!"

With a touch, she caused her chemise to fall to her feet, and stepped forward out of it in all her glorious nudity, the effect being heightened by the contrast caused by the triangular patch of tawny golden hair at the junction of her belly and thighs and her black silk stockings with their rose-tinted garters worn above the knees!

"This is how I meet my lover!" she said.

Martha became scarlet!

"How you are blushing, dear! Is it because of the sight of me standing naked? If so, you remind me of one of my girl friends who declares that the sight of me naked excites her much more than the sight of a naked man would do! Every time she comes to see me, she insists on my undressing myself completely in front of her! — and then you should see how she kisses and embraces me just as if she was playing with a naked man! Then she will go and do a thousand and one improper and indecent things to me which at first used to make me feel horribly ashamed, but which now I really like — even to the length of paying her back in the same coin! Oh! it's lovely! And mind you, we're not deceiving our husbands! Strange, but true! isn't it, eh?"

She kissed the blushing Martha, and continued?

"Ever since, I have had lovers and . . . enjoyed them; I still recollect how delicious those tête-à-tête with my girl friend were! We used to caress and kiss each others breasts, like this . . ."

"Oh! you're biting me!"

"Doesn't your lover do this to you? . . . Oh! see how the pretty little nipples are stiffening and standing out!"

"Oh! Madame, you're tickling me! . . . Oh! take away your hand! . . . Oh! what are you doing! . . . No! . . . no! . . . I don't want it!"

Mme de Liancourt had seized Martha and was passionately clasping her against herself, holding her tightly with one arm round her waist while she slipped her other hand between Martha's thighs! The latter, utterly surprised by this sudden attack, could only struggle feebly!

"Oh! . . . but Madame, what . . . are you going . . . to do . . . to me?"

"Make love with you, darling! I'm gone on you! Don't you know how one woman can adore another? — how two women can mutually prove their love for each other? — Let me show you! But you surely must know all about it! At school, didn't one of the bigger girls take charge of you, and teach you . . . this? Ah! — you're blushing now. Oh! you little humbug! . . ."

"That was so long ago! . . . I quite forget it all! . . ."

"No, one never forgets that sort of thing! Your girl friend must have had a sweet time! Come, dear little humbug, what was it you used to . . . do together? . . ."

"Really I don't know!"

"Really and truly? . . . Well, I know! . . . Come, you'd like to do it again, wouldn't you? . . . with me?"

"No, — no! Suppose . . . he came in! . . ."

"He can't, without our hearing him! . . . Come, you pretty little coward, come! Place yourself against me! . . . so! Take off your chemise! . . . you can have a dressing gown if you like!"

She gave Martha one.

"No, don't fasten it! . . . leave it quite open! . . . I want to have a good look at you! . . . your breasts — your belly — your hairs! . . . Oh! how they curl and cluster!''

Suddenly she knelt and applied her lips to the dark triangular patch that luxuriated at the end of Martha's stomach, the latter still offering a shame-faced resistance!

"No, no!" she cried, squeezing her legs closely together.

It had been however decreed and registered in the Book of Lesbian Venus that Mme de Liancourt should sacrifice yet another victim on the altar dedicated to tribadic love! I didn't think it was advisable to intervene! I felt sure that my turn would come before long, — and in the meantime here was Mme de Liancourt preparing for my delectation the most charming spectacle one could desire, one which the famous Regent would gladly have had performed before him at the Palais-Royal, yes, and paid cheerfully for it also!

Martha, now half-willing and still half-reluctantly, passively allowed herself to be placed on the sofa. Mme de Liancourt seated herself at Martha's side, passed one arm round her and slipped her other hand between Martha's thighs while she passionately kissed her, darting her tongue into Martha's mouth! Her finger, directed by both art and passion, soon produced the desired result! Martha's breath began to come brokenly, her eyes half closed, her bosom and breasts heaved agitatedly! At this moment Mme de Liancourt, no longer content to play only the part of the communicator of pleasure, caught hold of one of Martha's hands and gently conducted it to her own cunt with a mute demand for reciprocity! And Martha did not draw it back! — she recognised the silent request, and her gentle little hand began to do its untutored best!

What a charming picture the pair made! — what a glorious group worthy of Fragonard or of Boucher! I would have paid gladly a long price for a series of photographs representing them thus! Both girls intertwining their lovley white thighs and slender legs, then separating them only to interlace them in some other way in the midst of a storm of kisses and broken ejaculations, principally from Mme de Liancourt, who by now was simply mad with lust, her hips and haunches quivering, her body rapturously becoming more and more rigid!

"Martha! . . . oh darling! . . . keep on! . . . oh! . . . keep on! . . . You're . . . doing it . . . beautifully! . . . Oh! . . . Oh! . . . I'm coming! . . . Oh! . . . Oh! . . . I'm spending! . . . Ah! . . . a — h! . . ."

A moment of silence followed this ecstatic crisis, Mme de Liancourt still keeping her hand on Martha's slit!

"Oh! how wet you are! . . . You've also spent, you naughty thing! Darling, we've done it together! . . . Wipe yourself!" She gave Martha a handkerchief.

"Now, wasn't it good?"

"Yes!" replied Martha, timidly.

"Then let's do it together!"

"If you like!"

Immediately, our two lascivious heroines recommenced their lubricious caresses! Martha extended herself flat on her back on the sofa, and while her seducer, bending over her, looked her all over and felt and handled her as the spirit willed her, and freshly aroused in her new lust (as was manifest from the agitation of her bosom and breasts), Martha's hand, without invitation, stole to Mme de Liancourt's cunt and resumed its loving ministration. She had caught the fancy, she, so timid with me!

Nevertheless, she began to protest when, after having tenderly sucked her breasts, her mistress in lesbian pleasures carried her lips lower down!

"No, no, — not there!" she panted, trying to raise herself.

"Yes, yes! — I wish it! let me kiss your sweet cunny with its pretty hair! I'll do it just as well as your lover can!"

"But he has never . . . kissed me there!"

"Then he doesn't know his duties as your

lover! So much the better for me! I shall now be the first to do it to you! You'll see how delicious it is! I used to be just like you at first, — but now I simply adore this way! — and you'll always do it this way in future whenever you get the chance! . . . So! . . . Let me arrange you, open wider these pretty thighs! . . .

Then in the twinkling of an eye, the desired spot was covered with her lascivious and skilful mouth!

"No! no! . . . not there! . . . not down there! . . ." panted Martha as she felt Mme de Liancourt's tongue wandering over her cunt still virgin to such treatment and to the accompanying sensations!

For response, she was dragged down to the foot of the sofa, her thighs widely pulled apart, as Mme de Liancourt falling on her knees between them murmured almost unconsciously:

"Oh! what a lovely sweet fresh little cunny! . . . Oh! the beauty!" Then, like the swoop of hawk on a chicken, her mouth attacked it and remained there as if glued to it! Completely defeated, Martha fell on her back again and resigned herself as best she could to abandon herself to the voluptuous sensations that now were thrilling through her, induced by the ardent tongue of her passionate friend! Some minutes thus passed! At last Mme de Liancourt raised herself, red, flushed, panting, almost delirious!

"Together? . . . together? . . . Will you? . . ."

"What?" gasped Martha.

"This! . . . Let's do it together! . . . Will you? . . ."

"If you wish it! . . . But how? . . ."

"I'll show you, darling! . . . Now watch!"

She got on the sofa, turned her bottom towards Martha's head, straddled across Martha, then placed herself astride of her face, her belly resting on Martha's breasts and her cunt seeking the same lingual caress which she was recommencing on Martha's one now lying below her lips. Her thighs hid half the face of my sweet little mistress, and I could only see a bit of her forehead and her pretty hair emerge from between Mme de Liancourt's buttocks. As the latter wriggled and waggled her charming globes of flesh in lascivious undulations, I noted that Martha had accommodated herself to her position, and that her mouth as docilely as her hand comprehended and daintily executed the delicate function demanded from it!

But as for Mme de Liancourt, she was simply mad with passionate lust! What a strange thing it is that a woman can thus procure for herself such keen and ecstatic enjoyment in thus caressing another woman! I was splendidly placed for contemplating her, — and also the object of her delirious worship! I saw her face in profile, her chin resting on the hairs, her mouth poised on the lips of Martha's slit between which her tongue was playing! These secret charms of Martha, hitherto unknown to me, made me envy Mme de Liancourt both her place and the game she was playing! Time after time I was on the point of bursting out of my hiding place, and planting my mouth on the sweet spot she was attacking! — (our convention would have authorised the act) but I refrained! The charm of the spectacle fascinated me!

Sometimes Mme de Liancourt seemed as if she wanted to get the whole of Martha's cunt into her mouth! — sometimes amused herself by administering little touches to the clitoris with her tongue! — then she would pass her tongue right along the tender slit from top to bottom, — sometimes she would, with her fingers, separate the sensitive lips and thrust her tongue between them as deeply as she possibly could! Frequently she stopped, inspected attentively the sweet object of her admiration with eyes blazing with lust unsatisfied, then ejaculating frenziedly in her passionate adoration. "Oh! this cunt! . . . this sweet cunt! . . . this delicious darling cunt! . . ." She would shower kisses on it! How Martha must have revelled in bliss! I would have liked to have been able to watch her tell-tale face! She evidently was acquitting herself most satisfactorily in reciprocating Mme de Liancourt's attentions, if one might judge by the plungings and joggings of the latter's body as she brokenly ejaculated. "Oh! . . . oh! . . . you do it well! . . . I can feel your tongue! . . . now, do you feel mine? . . . wait . . . I'm going to shove it right inside this sweet cunt . . . as far in . . . as . . . it will go . . . There! . . ."

It is impossible to indicate the accent of these words as pronounced by a mouth the tongue of which was endeavouring to talk and lick at one and the same moment! What a terrible state of nervous excitement must have possessed Mme de Liancourt, a woman so reserved and correct in ordinary life, especially in language! But the ecstatic crisis was fast approaching! . . . the breathings became more and more broken!

"Martha . . . oh! Martha! . . . oh! darling . . . I'm coming! . . . Ah! . . . Ah! . . . I'm spending! . . . are you? . . . spend! . . . together! . . . wait a moment! . . . now! . . . now! . . . Oh! . . . I'm spending . . . again! . . . spend also! . . . s.p.e.n.d!!!"

Their bodies stiffened, constricted, — I heard a deep sigh of unspeakable pleasures! . . . They had finished!

Mme de Liancourt slowly slipped off her position and then proceeded to give her pupil kiss after kiss of approbation and satisfaction.

"Darling! your face is all wet with what you have drawn out of me! . . . And I've drunk you! . . . Use my handkerchief! . . . How flushed and red you are! . . . Now, wasn't it good?"

"Oh! yes . . . much better than I could have believed!"

Was it not now time for me to put in an appearance? But what could I do with two women whose lust had thus been satiated! Nevertheless I decided to show myself, and opened the door, regretting that I had delayed so long!

Two piercing cries saluted me! Martha leaped on her piled up garments and covered herself as best she could with the first she could snatch, then hid herself behind the bed curtains Mme de Liancourt caught up a velvet mantle trimmed with fur and threw it hastily round her, but it reached only to her fleshy buttocks and did not even cover the fur of her belly.

"What do you mean, sir," she exclaimed with a fine pretence of anger and outraged modesty, — "what do you mean by thus rushing into a lady's room without first knocking? It is a piece of the greatest impertinence! You are a mannerless brute! . . . You might well have waited! We were changing our dresses so that we might with the greatest safety leave the house! I had forgotten to lock the door, — but I really considered you knew better . . ."

"Madame, I humbly and earnestly beg your pardon for having surprised you in this way," I replied suppressing as best I could the desire to laugh — "but I came in trusting in your promise to give a kind refuge to this lady and myself!"

"Yes! — but Madame has been waiting for you for some time now; we had given you up! Is this your idea of the proper way of keeping an appointment? But I will abide by my promise; you can have my room and my bed. Only be prudent! I know your secrets now and if I choose I can be nasty!"

She winked at me out of the corner of her eye as if to qualify her menace, then walked past me towards her dressing-room.

"Take care about the sheets!" she added with a meaningly wicked smile!

I watched as she walked her lovely plump and round bottom, quivering and waggling with every step, — I would dearly have liked to have put myself into her! But I went and dragged Martha out of her hiding place.

"What makes you so red, dear?"

"I've been laughing so much! Madame has been telling me the funniest stories . . ."

"You look simply charming in that dressing gown! — but don't fasten it up, it's quite unnecessary!"

"Oh! . . . very well. But wait a minute. Don't look!"

She disappeared into the lavatory, and while she was engaged in clearing away all traces of her recent pranks, I undressed myself; then when she re-appeared I took her in my arms and carried her to the bed, on which I gently laid her. Her desires which I had feared were by now dormant were quickly restored to life again, having another promise of satisfaction in a different way! Her modesty after so rude an experience had become less troublesome, — and I did not meet with any marked resistance on her part when after bestowing a thousand kisses all over her body, I did to her what Mme de Liancourt had so sweetly inaugurated — the deliciousness of which she now fully appreciated as with her two little hands she pressed my face against her slit so as not to lose a single movement of my tongue!

I thought of Mme de Liancourt, and wished she could see us! But she did even better than this; she stood stark-naked by the side of the bed and while I was busy between Martha's thighs, she kissed her lips and squeezed her breasts, — while the former, having within her reach her friend's thighs, slipped her hand between them and let it disappear under the plentiful cluster of curling hairs, without interrupting my ministrations.

Excited, inflamed, burning with hot desire, I

rose to throw myself on Martha and quench in her the fire that was raging in my veins! But at that moment Mme de Liancourt carried her hand to the lowest point of my belly and seized the object she found there in a state of furious erection!

"Look, Martha!" she exclaimed, "look at it! Have you ever seen it before? isn't it splendid! See, how stiff it is! — that's in honour of you, my dear! Oh! I must . . . I can't help it! . . ."

I was then kneeling on the bed. With a single quick movement she seated herself with her head at the required height, — then covered with hot kisses my member which she found just on a level with her lips. She kissed and re-kissed the gland, the hairs, the testicles, murmuring endearments, then she took my prick into her mouth and sucked it madly in front of Martha, who in utter astonishment was watching her!

"Now, Martha, you take it, — it's your turn! Suck it! Do as I did!"

"I don't know how to!" stammered Martha, — it's so big!"

Now redder than fire she approached it, kissed the tip and tried for some time in vain to take it into her mouth — when all of a sudden it slipped in, as if in spite of her, completely filling her mouth, and she then proceeded to suck me violently! Oh! my raptures! It was Martha! Martha herself that was sucking me! It was not with the lascivious skill of Mme de Liancourt, — but her inexperience itself gave to her caress a special and indescribable spice of pleasure!

Finally I put Martha flat on the back, — I let myself fall between her arms and legs, and shoved my prick into her burning cunt! — tasting delights hitherto unknown, divine, delirious! Already I could see Martha's eyes slowly turning upwards and half-closing, indicating her approaching ecstasy — when Mme de Liancourt, no doubt jealous of our transports, put herself astride across Martha's face, blindly seeking for her cunt a further caress which it was impossible to refuse to her! Being thus suddenly driven away from Martha's lips and tongue I transferred my kisses to the two luscious globes of flesh which I had at my mouth's command, kissing them, nibbling and playfully biting them in spite of their squirming and constant agitation!

Dear readers, I will confess that my tongue at times lost itself in the furrow which separated these temptingly superb buttocks, so much did the sight of them and the subtle perfume which emanated from them madden me!

But everything must end! We three spent simultaneously! The blissful ejaculations of sperm calmed us! One by one we came to our senses and rose to purify and refresh ourselves!

"My gracious! I've got it all over me!" cried

Martha in pretty confusion, — "even on my stockings! . . . they're quite wet!"

"Well, dear," said Mme de Liancourt to her, you've done very well for one time! You must be very tired! By the time you get home, your eyes will have dark rings round them, — and then what will your husband think, eh?"

"Ah! I'll risk that! That won't stop me from . . . doing it again."

"What, today?"

"Why not? . . . When one has tasted the forbidden fruit, one must bite it well!" she replied, dropping her eyes. "Now I know what it is to be libertine! And I fancy it won't be long before I am nearly as clever at this game as Madame, your old pupil, with whom you evidently have been practising, eh?"

"How do you know?"

"By this!" she replied, pointing to an article that stood on the toilet table, which she and I had bought together and which I had left at Mme de Liancourt's.

"But I didn't want this proof after what I have seen today!" Martha continued chaffingly, — now if I had been jealous . . ."

"Your jealousy would have deprived us from the delicious time we have had together!" replied Mme de Liancourt.

"I quite agree with you!" said Martha with a

smile.

Mme de Liancourt showed herself a good teacher, and rapidly she educated her apt pupil, till it only remained to put her lessons into practice and delight her "amant" and her "amante"! And after the cares of the toilet had been attended to and a few glasses of champagne taken, we arranged that all three should meet at Mme de Liancourt's chambers on the first day that Martha was able to come, and we separated with longing for the time when we should next find ourselves in Mme de Liancourt's delicious boudoir for a *séance à trois!*

_____

# III

On a warm summer morning, a young lady of elegant appearance was strolling in a pretty park, selecting the narrower paths when possible and every now and then looking behind her over her shoulder as if she was on the way to some love-tryst and feared that she might be followed. As a matter of fact she was being followed by a gentleman who did not lose sight of her for a single minute as he slipped along, hiding himself in the brushwood like an Indian in a jungle!

My fair readers, do I hear you say, what is he going to relate to us? — a scene of jealousy? — a husband surprising his wife just as she is about to enjoy with the sweet help of her lover a supplement to the monotonous conjugal attentions?

103

Oh no! Please be reassured! Should anything drip it certainly won't be blood, — and if you should be affected by the fortune of our heroine it will be only with the most delicious of emotions!

The young lady quietly made her way to a sort of summer-house, then after a final look round she picked up her skirts (thereby revealing prettily shod feet and shapely calves), pressed through the surrounding herbage to the door, opened it quickly and disappeared within.

*Sic vos non vobis . . .*

For it was no other than myself who was thus taking a share in this adventure, a poacher in conjugal preserves!

Since I first met Mme de Baisieux in Paris and obtained an introduction to her, and above all at the Chateau de C... when kind fortune had made us guests together, I had made assiduous siege to her with a certain hope of success as her husband was away on a long sea trip. But up to date I had been frustrated, — and now my want of success seemed to be explained, the place I desired was already occupied!

I thought of withdrawing, but I wished first to make certain of the position; and may I confess that I was also seized with the desire of being a spectator of the piquant scene which no doubt was about to take place and which would finally and convincingly show me the uselessness of further pursuit.

"How shocking!" my lady readers will no doubt exclaim! Well, perhaps so, but I ask them to deal not too hardly with me in a matter of curiosity!

Thereupon I sought for the means of seeing without being seen. A little garret-window afforded me the desired assistance, and through it I obtained a view of the interior, full of hay, a suitable furnishing to a rustic boudoir. Mme de Baisieux was still alone; after having carefully closed the door, she seemed to be choosing a suitable spot for the sacrifice. I held my breath in my absorbed attention, quivering at the idea of being able to witness the scene which the principal actress was preparing against the arrival of the leading actor. Only I could not understand why she had so carefully fastened the door!

As soon as she had found a suitable place, Mme de Baisieux seated herself, took out of her pocket a little book and hurriedly turned over the pages. At last she seemed to find what she was seeking. Forcing the book open so that she could easily hold it so in one hand, she stretched herself out voluptuously, supported herself on her elbow, — while her disengaged hand . . .

My dear lady readers, have you guessed? Need I draw a curtain over a picture which you all must recognise? Will you not prefer to take a naughty peep at the sin your sister is about to commit?

This hand with a graceful movement raised her dress and the white petticoats beneath it. In consequence of the heat, she had not put on any drawers, and so my eager eyes were able to travel delightedly over all the charms I so ardently coveted but which so far I did not possess! And all I saw only inflamed me all the more, — for her charming exterior had not lied and her naked person was all and more than all I anticipated would be found under her clothes. All was rounded, plump! Above the dainty shoe came a slender shapely leg with a delicately rounded calf, a neat knee, then higher up a thigh underlined prettily by her blue garter, — the whole issuing from out of a wave of lace frillings! A fold of her chemise had dropped and so hid the part to which her hand had stolen! It was a living representation of Boilly's picture "MIDI" only with all the movement in it!

So far I had never been privileged to witness this solitary feminine pastime! It was therefore with strangely concentrated attention that I followed every movement of her hand — as it first began to rove from one end to the other of her slit, sweetly and caressingly, as if to gently flatter and excite the deity it sought to tame.

She read a few lines, — then her movements quickened! There was a gentle tremble, as if a tremolo was being executed on the charming instrument on which she was playing, — then quicker, and still more quickly . . . The book slipped out of her hand . . . her body and her head fell back . . . her eyes half closed, showing the whites . . . while her lips half opened, displaying her pearly teeth . . .

Between her widely extended legs her hand continued its tender gymnastics. She jerked her stomach upwards in violent up-heavings, which allowed me momentary glances of blond clustering hairs, but not of the dainty tickling finger which had been entrusted with the delicate mission of awaking and exciting the sources of her pleasure . . . Ah! now it was over . . . the delicious crisis had come and gone!

Mme de Baisieux raised herself, put the precious book into her pocket, brushed the dust off her garments, inspected herself in a pocket mirror, — and satisfied with the result, slipped prudently and cautiously away.

I quitted my peep-hole in a state of excitement more easily understood than described. My brain seethed with fresh desires and with them the hope of being able to enjoy them in the company of her whom I coveted, all the more so as it was evident now that she had no means of obtaining for herself a more solid and satisfactory way of solace.

I made a long round in the park timing myself

so as to meet her on one of the pathways where she was amusing herself with plucking wild flowers. The action was natural enough as was our meeting, nevertheless she blushed, — for a woman will betray herself thus under such conditions. And she was not any more at her ease when I remarked that she was looking pale and tired. All the evening, I harped on this theme, leading her to think that I suspected her of having kept an amorous rendez-vous, a teasing she accepted in good temper in the impression that she had completely thrown me off the scent as to her real occupation of the morning. Nevertheless, it was many days before she went out by herself. Was this the result of distrust, or prudence, — or was she able to solace herself in the house? I learnt the truth later on; the poor girl occupied a room that communicated with that of the lady who owned the house, her aunt, — and it was a regular school-girl's room in which she had no privacy whatever; hence her visits to the summer house.

The recollection of my delicious vision was always with me.

I dearly would have loved to have witnessed again the charming scene, to plan so that I could turn up at precisely the right moment, — at all events to get a chance of a talk with her by ourselves!

One day, the owner of a neighbouring estate invited the gentlemen of our party to his place for some rabbit shooting. I loved the sport, but what were my feelings of regret that I had accepted the invitation, when I saw that Mme de Baisieux, strawhatted, was on the point of going out by herself while we were filling our cartridge pouches! Hardly had we started, when I pretended that I had forgot mine (as a mere pretence for getting back to the house).

"We'll lend you some," my friends exclaimed.

"They won't do," I explained, — "I use no. 12."

"I believe I saw the gentleman place his cartridge pouch in the waggon," said a servant.

The gentleman had carefully taken them out again quietly!

"Shall we wait for you?"

"No, no, — I'll follow on foot. Begin without me. You may as well take my gun along with yours though."

Off they all went! And now for the park!

The summer-house had its back on the wall of the roadway. I took the quickest cut to it by not entering the park by the side gate, and soon I was at the gable end. Perhaps Mme de Baisieux had already begun to . . . to . . .! In a desperate hurry, I scrambled over the wall and jumped down on the other side.

Crack went something! Oh, bad luck! A confounded nail had caught in my breeches and had ripped one leg open from waistband to knee! And I wasn't wearing drawers! What was I to do!

Just then, I caught sight of Mme de Baisieux at the foot of the little slope on which the summerhouse stood, evidently making her way to it. She was leading her little cousin by the hand, from which I came to the conclusion that she did not propose today to satisfy the cravings of sexual desire. — I was rather pleased than otherwise, for now I could slip in and hide there till the evening or until I managed in some way to mend my torn breeches.

So in I slipped, and was hardly among the bundles of hay and certainly not full of voluptuous ideas, when the door suddenly opened, and I saw Mme de Baisieux enter, leaving the little child outside.

"Don't you come in," she said, — "I'm going to see if there are any rats here and to kill them. So don't come in, for they may bite you."

"Don't be long, cousin!"

"No, no." And she set to work to find the spot she occupied on the last occasion.

I had taken off my breeches and I had them in my hand, greatly embarrassed. Here was the much desired *tête-à-tête*, and a stupid accident was preventing me from benefiting by it! But the

110

sight of Mme de Baisieux, looking more charming than ever inspired me with the most voluptuous ideas and re-aminated my somewhat chilled desires and gave me the necessary audacity that the situation demanded. The recollection of the charms which I could still imagine under her clothes and which I perhaps was again going to see in their lovely nudity soon produced on me the effect that no pretty woman can help producing on any man worthy of the name. Rather than appear after the conclusion of the little play she was preparing for herself (and which would make her die of shame if she thought I had been a spectator of her actions) I showed myself without further delay.

A cry of startled modesty, quite natural, greeted me.

"What are you doing here, Monsieur? — I thought you had gone off with the shooting party!"

"I did start with them, but I left my cartridges behind and came back for them, — and chose the quickest way; and in climbing over the garden wall I have torn my breeches badly. I saw you coming along and so took refuge here, — and was horribly astonished when you came in! Now will you do me a great favour? Can you somehow get me a needle and thread so that I can repair this disaster as far as may be possible, at all events sufficiently to allow of my getting out of my present extremely unfortunate and inconvenient position!"

Mme de Baisieux broke into hearty laughter, no doubt relieved to find that I had not been spying on her; my accident thus saved me from suspicions which would have entirely spoiled my chances!

Briefly, so as not to tire my readers with conversations and explanations, after some hesitation on Mme de Baisieux's part, we arranged that I should hide in a corner and throw my breeches over to her; she then would mend them as much as possible and throw them back to me. She had the necessary needle and thread with her and in a few minutes she completed her work.

"There you are, Monsieur," she exclaimed as she threw the breeches back to me, and which I quickly slipped on, — "now good morning!"

"Oh please, wait a moment to let me thank you!"

"No, no. — good-bye! If any one should find us together here! . . ."

But by this time, I was alongside of her and had slipped my arm round her waist while I begged for a sweet kiss! — I then stole one.

"Enough! enough! no more!" she protested, — suppose any one should come in! . . . And my cousin?"

"Only one word, please! I must tell you!"

"Quickly then!"

"I didn't scramble over the wall to get my cartridges, — I wanted to get here without exciting anyone's suspicions, for I saw you on your way here. I wanted to tell you that you are the prettiest girl I know, that I adore you . . ." And I rained kisses on her cheeks.

"Oh! oh! — Monsieur Henri, how can you! . . . I couldn't have believed it . . ."

"I adore you! you are so pretty, so sweet! Oh! Bertha, my darling, my love! . . . you will? . . . — you will? . . . won't you? . . ."

"What! . . . do you know my name?"

"It's the first thing a man learns about the girl he loves, — and I've known it for a long time!"

All the time I continued to shower kisses on her as I held her tightly clasped in my arms against me. I could feel how her flesh was quivering through her thin summer dress, as I covered her cheeks, the nape of her neck, her throat, her mouth and lips with my ardent kisses. She let herself sink down on the straw murmuring "Enough! . . . enough! . . ." then, as if to conceal her surrender of herself now commencing, she fell into a half-swoon, closing her eyes which I kissed, and half-opening her lips, between which my tongue promptly slipped without however getting any reciprocal response from hers! One of my arms supported her body, the other hand crept under her dress and petticoats and caressed gently her dainty calves, then after a pause crept higher up to her garters where when a woman's leg is bent one can so deliciously lodge one's hand between the swell of the calf and the skin of the thigh! From this point of vantage, getting bolder, my hand crept still higher! Oh! what a sweet thrill ran through both of us when my fingers touched the soft warm bare flesh of her plump rounded thighs which she was vainly squeezing against each other.

This time also she had no drawers on! From the top of her dainty shoes to her smooth satin belly, the hairs on which I now gently was playing with, there was no obstacle to my full view!

"No! . . . no! . . ." she murmured as she felt my fingers invade her slit, — "not there! . . . not there! . . ."

But in spite of this flicker of rebellion, this last effort of expiring shame, my finger settled itself on her tiny clitoris and commenced the ecstatic function which Mme de Baisieux hitherto had reserved for her own little fingers! Under its sweetly mysterious influence, her body began to stretch itself out, her faintness increased, her tongue began to respond to mine! And then her legs commenced to open out! She was mine! — she had surrendered herself to me! — I now only had to take possession of her!

In one's first amorous encounter with any fresh woman, it is always most advisable that one should go slowly at first, watching her carefully and defeating every attempt at resistance, — to pretend to be seized with delirious passion for her — until your sweet combatant yields herself under the repeated thrills of pleasure you have communicated to her, — then let yourself go and indulge to the utmost your concupiscence and your desires.

I was now burning to look closely at all the charms that so far I had seen from a distance only. Quickly I threw up her clothes so as to get a good look — and as I did I thought of the piquant spectacle we would afford any one who might have his eye where I had mine on the previous occasion!

All I saw were now mine! . . . mine! these lovely legs, these slender, dainty calves. She was wearing the same underclothing as on the last occasion, — tiny kid-shoes, cream-coloured silk stockings, blue garters. On her right thigh was a tiny brown molemark! Oh! how I longed to kiss everything! — that lovely satin skin, that silky chestnut triangular patch of curls which formed so adorable a contrast to her blonde beauty! — how I would have liked to put my mouth on the delicious little slit which was now beginning to open its pouting lips! But I hadn't the time now! I had to keep holding her clothes up! Another time I would repay myself with interest!

Recalled thus to the sweet reality, I placed myself between her charming legs, I pulled her clothes still higher up, I rapidly undid the front of my breeches and freed my imprisoned member — then shoved it still and burning into the sweet opening that was impatiently awaiting its introduction, — while at the same time I thrust my tongue as deeply as I could into the mouth of my pretty victim.

"Bertha! . . . oh! Bertha! . . . oh! how heavenly! . . . your're delicious! . . . divine! . . . oh! you angel! . . . you angel! . . ."

Women as a rule do not let their lovers who are rogering them for the first time understand how they appreciate the pleasure that is wildly rioting through them all the time, for they love to behave as if they were being violated! Mme de Baisieux only departed from this policy to murmur as we were approaching the sweet ecstatic conclusion. "Oh! . . . please . . . please . . . take it out! . . . not inside me! . . . no! no! please!" Although I was mad with pleasure I had sufficient control of myself to obey her. Unfortunate results might otherwise arise from our pleasure. Oh! mysterious decrees of Providence! — without you how much more amiable and obliging women would be, — and also how deliciously libertine!

It comes back to me how I was kissing her tiny ear ornamented with a single pearl as I awaited the moment when I must withdraw my prick from inside her in accordance with her prudent request. The moment arrived, — everything shot on to her white petticoat!

I offered her my handkerchief.

"But then you won't have a handkerchief!" she exclaimed.

"Oh, yes! — I'll preserve it in memory of the delicious use you will have made of it!" I replied with a smile. She blushed prettily.

While we were exchanging the loving kisses which follow so tender an encounter, we heard a little voice at the door!

"Cousin, cousin, haven't you finished killing the rats yet?" We had absolutely forgotten all about the child that was patiently waiting outside!

"Yes, yes!" called out my lovely companion raising herself hurriedly and flushing scarlet — "I'm just coming! — I've killed the last I think!"

We couldn't maintain our seriousness at the plaintive trouble in the little voice that had thus interrupted us.

"Here I am, dear, I'm just coming. Don't come in!"

"Good-bye Bertha, my darling!" I whispered, — when again?"

"Oh! — never, never!"

"You little humbug! Shall we say tomorrow?"

"No, no! . . . I'll tell you, later!"

"One last kiss then!" She gave me a delicious one in which her tongue and mine also said goodbye! "Now goodbye! . . . *Au revoir!*"

As she neared the door, she brushed and dusted herself, took a glance in a pocket mirror she had with her, waved her hand lovingly to me, said goodbye again with her eyes, — then slipped out.

As soon as I considered she would got to a safe distance, I in my turn crept out, hurried off to my bedroom and quickly changed my things, as they carried evident traces of our sweet combat! Then I picked up my cartridge pouch and set off to rejoin the shooting party, my absence being hardly an hour. How one can employ time sometimes!

From that day, for Mme de Baisieux and me, the term *to kill a rat* became synonymous with "have a turn". In spite of her innocent air, she was full of mischief, and did not hesitate to let herself loose in her love-letters to me. In memory of the adventure she adopted the following formula in her *billets-doux*.

"Mon cher Monsieur, will you give the pleasure of your company at a rat hunt on . . . next at the usual place." She continuted to send me these invitations after we had returned to Paris, even when her husband was there; he did not stay there long, but his presence nevertheless was a nuisance as it of necessity reduced the frequency of our "hunts" and the consequent opportunities of satisfying our desires!

When our liaison had become very intimate I told her that one day I had surprised her in the act of "frigging" herself! I was sweetly scolded for thus playing the spy on a "poor lone woman", but I was soon pardoned, and she consented to let me see the book which seemed to arouse the desires which she strove thus to satisfy. She had found it among her brother's papers. It was *The Confessions of a Woman of the "World"*, illustrated in the most lascivious way, — enough to excite anyone's senses!

"On the day we first killed the rat, what bit were you reading?" I asked softly.

In pretty embarrassment she pointed out to me the following lines, which we then read together:

"As I lay on my back on my sofa, stretched out at full length with my legs widely parted, my lover fell on his knees in front of me and in the most delicious way sucked me till I spent in thrilling delirium!"

Needless to say we did not read any more that day! And I take this opportunity to express to the amiable author and to his clever illustrator my sincere thanks for having thus aroused a fire which I was able to extinguish in the pleasantest way possible!

## IV

If from time immemorial the French woman, especially the Parisienne, has enjoyed the reputation of being in love affairs the most agreeable and the most sprightly of her sex, and of knowing how to impart to her favours a piquancy which greatly augments their value, I venture to consider that the Vienna ladies should be allowed to participate in this praise, especially such as have had the benefit of Parisian education, — for their elegance, their air of distinction, their coquetry, their talent for being discreetly provoking, in no way ranks behind their Parisian sisters whom often they surpass in beauty of form and figure. Full of curiosity in all matters appertaining to sexual love, they delight to make a study of them and to lose themselves in dream eroticism, in meditations of the most refined lubricity, — after which they will resume in the easiest manner possible the outward appearance of the most virtuous and well-behaved woman.

Such at all events was Mme de Schoenfutz. Transplanted from the banks of the Danube to those of the Seine, she had there found so many subjects for amorous study that she did not long live in accord with her legal lord and master; the latter, like a wise man, avoided any scandal by quietly letting her live as she chose while he in turn did as he also pleased.

It was I who was the privileged mortal with whom she took her first lessons in the Art of Love, with whom she made her first studies, — which we did not hesitate to carry on to extremes!

She was a delicious pupil, so full of enthusiasm! I could conduct her and teach her the most outrageous method of unrestrained lust as long as I did so by agreeable and picturesquely amusing paths! — and there was little doubt that I had hit off the right way, as very soon she became most expert!

But everything comes to an end, even such delightful refinements of amorous pleasure. She began to put into practice with others the lessons I had taught her, — while I passed on to the education of other pupils. Since then we had often met — but Our Lady Venus did not receive any sweet sacrifice from us, partly because the occasions were not propitious and time was wanting. Now the attractions of the hunting season had brought us together at the Château de V . . .

My Viennese charmer had become even more beautiful than before; to the charms of her face and figure was now added a certain trick in the way she looked at you, which under the air of distinction nevertheless indicated she was not wanting either in enterprise or audacity. In short I found myself ready if she should indicate that she was willing. But do not think that I imagined that I had only to ask her to let me have (so to speak) my latchkey again. — To have done so would have been both foolish and fatal, for a woman requires to be re-conquered by any man whose caresses she has forgotten. Accordingly I laid siege to her in the regular way, but at first all the encouragement I got lay in vague half-promises, such as "Perhaps! . . . if you're very good!" But little by little I made progress, — now snatching a hasty kiss, now a significant pressure of her corsage, sometimes a hand slipped under her clothes but not permitted to! . . .

One day, we went out fox-hunting. Mme de Schoenfutz both rode well and looked well on horse-back, having something of the elegance of seat and style of the late Empress Elizabeth of Austria, whom indeed she resembled in more ways than one.

The atmosphere was heavy and thunderous, the heat stifling. The sport was poor. Twice the hounds had to be whipped off a false scent. A state of confusion prevailed, and the riders formed little groups as they watched the proceedings and held themselves ready to gallop off as soon as the signal was given. Presently the sky began to be covered with black threatening clouds which presaged a serious storm. Was it good enough to go on? — wouldn't it be as well to get shelter? But before any general decision was arrived at, a roll of thunder shook the air and large drops of rain began to fall.

Immediately there was a general skedaddle, — a wild rush for the carriages. Several riders galloped off to the kennels not far off, others to the village of T... The men ceased to chat with their lady friends and with each other, concerned now to make the best of their way to shelter. But M. de Z. (who I suspected to be in Mme de Schoenfutz's high favour) remained by her and asked her what she proposed to do.

"I'm going back home," she said.

"You'd much better come to T..., the rain will soon be over and we can then resume hunting."

"Many thanks! in the forest, all dripping! I've

had enough for one day already!"

"But really it is not going to be wet."

"Please don't let me keep you from hunting!
I'm going off, I hate rain!"

"Then let me come with you! You don't know
the road and you will most likely take the longest
way round . . ."

But Mme de Schoenfutz had galloped off as he
spoke! And now I recognised why old Ovid had
included the chase among his Remedies for Love!
M. de Z . . . did not insist on following. The lady
riders all dismounted quickly and crowded into
carriages to drive back to the Château, while the
men unanimously allowed them to go off un-
escorted while they themselves made the best of
their way to T . . . to wait there till the rain was
over and the hunt could be resumed.

"This is much jollier than with all those petticoats hanging about!" remarked F . . ., a woman-
hating sportsman. "Come along to T . . . — there's
a good hotel there, a good stable, and a good
billiard table on which we can have a game while
we wait."

"Sorry I can't come, old chap," I replied, — "I
must go off to see one of the keepers about a dog.
We'll meet presently."

It had stopped raining, but the sky was more
threatening than ever. My intention was not to
stop at the keeper's but to get off to the Château

and try and find Mme de Schoenfutz, — for in such panics, it is seldom that an enterprising gallant does not have some luck, because everybody is too busy looking after himself or herself to notice what any one else is doing. So after a few minutes at the keeper's house, I galloped down a bridle path which was a short cut to the Château and led into the road Mme de Schoenfutz had taken.

As I joined the road I saw some way down a lady riding slowly by herself. It was she! I soon caught her up.

"What! not home yet?" I exclaimed.

"No," she replied, "My horse has a stone in his hoof and I have nothing to get it out with. So I am forced to go slowly."

I had with me the necessary implement and soon put matters right, then remounted.

"Are they all coming this way?" she asked.

"Yes, the carriages are just behind, with all the women inside them."

"Then let us get out of their way, — for if they see me with you after the way I rushed off, they will conclude that our meeting was premeditated."

"You are quite right! Let us ride down here."

As soon as we had got out of sight of any one on the road, I drew alongside my fair companion and slipped my arm round her slender waist, then drawing her quickly to me I kissed her lips ardently.

"Enough! . . . enough!" she exclaimed, trying to release herself, "here comes the rain!"

"I don't mind the rain as long as I have you!" And I renewed my amorous assault, clasping her passionately against me as I kissed her furiously, darting my tongue into her mouth, squeezing her waist with one hand while the other attacked her bosom, her knees, her thighs which I felt and pressed through the cloth of her habit. So impetuous was my attack that I nearly caused her to fall off her horse.

"Oh! . . . oh! . . . what are you doing! — is it the storm that has made you so mad?"

"Yes! . . . yes! a storm of love and desire! I am full of love's electricity, like the clouds."

"And so you want me to be your lightning-conductor! but I thought I had become incapable of electrifying you to such an extent."

"You know well that you are to me what no other woman can be. And if you would like a proof of your power over me . . ."

"As a matter of fact, folk that have known of our old liaison suspect me now to be with any one but you."

"But you haven't answered my question! Do let us take advantage of our security! Let me prove to you that you have electrified me to the uttermost of my capacity! Will you? . . . may I? . . ."

"Well . . . yes! . . . but you're not allowing for the storm!"

As a matter of fact the rain now had begun to come down heavily, rain that clears the air but which is a horrible nuisance to an out-of-doors *rendez-vous* without any curtains beyond the kindly trees!

We went off at a gallop down the path. Was it never coming to an end? Soon I noticed that we were going away from our proper course, the fault of our hasty flight. I was somewhat upset by this, but said nothing. We continued to gallop. Presently a signpost came in sight, I rode up to it — the château was a good three miles from where we were.

"Where are we?" she asked.

"Oh, not far off."

"Then which is the road? This way?"

Just then I caught sight of a shanty (or hut) hidden in the forest. It was a sort of hunting shelter with a lean-to for the horses. The sight put a droll idea into my mind, — here was a nest for an amorous pair!

At all events, it would be only prudent to avail ourselves of this unexpected shelter. We tied the horses under the lean-to, and forcing open the locked door we went inside. We found ourselves in a fair sized room, quite bare except for one or two strawseated chairs and a fireplace. In the ceiling there was a trap door which evidently communicated with a hay-loft.

Hardly had we entered when the rain began to come down in torrents. What we had experienced was nothing to what was now falling, a veritable deluge! I kindled a fine fire in the hearth with the debris and straw I found lying about, — then I took off my coat and hung it across the back of a chair in front of the fire. Mme de Schoenfutz slipped out of her riding-habit and did the same.

She looked deliciously piquant as she stood thus, décolletée, her pretty arms bare, with her riding-breeches, her dainty riding-boots and little man's silk hat!

I gently caught hold of her and drew her against me, — then slipped my hand under her chemisette and getting hold of one of her round full breasts, I drew it out of its hiding place and kissed it passionately. "Suppose some one should come!" she whispered.

"Wait a moment!" I replied, and went out. I brought the horses inside, then barricaded the door, — now no one could possibly suspect our presence, for even the fire (now reduced to a glowing mass) did not throw off any smoke to call attention to human habitation.

"Now we're at home!"

Seated on a chair with Mme de Schoenfutz on my knee, I surrendered myself to my desires! On her part she abandoned herself entirely to me, returning me kiss for kiss, laughing delightedly at the originality of our situation. She simply adored such situations! By now I had pulled both of her sweet little breasts out of her corset and was kissing them fiercely, — under my burning lips, the pretty little nipples began to swell up and get hard.

"I really believe they recognise you!" she said laughingly.

"Then what about my third little friend, the sweetest, the sauciest, the wickedest of them all!" — and my fingers unbuttoned the front of her riding breeches and slipped inside!

"It's an odd sensation," I remarked maliciously, "to find a cunt inside a man's breeches!" And my happy hand set to work to caress and play with the sweet feminine hairs it found, then stole between a pair of soft plump satin-like thighs which it felt and handled, — and then my finger made its way into a certain opening already warm and moist and commenced to play on her little quivering clitoris! . . .

As her pleasure crept over her, my pretty companion began to become sweetly agitated. Her hand stole towards me; I delightedly guided it. Quickly unbuttoning my trousers I helped her to drag out what she was seeking and what she now had got hold of!

"Just suppose that you had found something like this when you put your hand inside my riding breeches!" she remarked laughingly.

"What an idea!"

"He recognises me, I'm sure! He wants to see his old friend!"

The way in which we had placed ourselves was not propitious or convenient for the prosecution of our adventures. True pleasure demands horizontal position, — and I, at all events, consider that one only cheats Venus if one sacrifices to her in the odd positions which are only allowable when there is absolutely no help for it. So instead of making her sit astride on my knees (as she seemed to expect) I suggested that I should climb into the hayloft to see whether we could not build for ourselves a more comfortable nest up there.

The ladder was rather ricketty, — however I got up all right. The loft was full of hay, sweet-smelling. I quickly persuaded Mme de Schoen-futz to join me, — but as the ladder was a little short for her I had some little difficulty in raising her off it, she all the time laughing and revelling in the adventure.

"Now, where?" she asked, looking about her.

O delicious question, "Now, where?" As much as to say "where shall I place myself so as to let you have me, — to yield myself to you — to let you do whatever you like to me!"

I collected some bundles of hay and soon improvised as excellent couch on to which I gently placed her.

"The mice will see us!" she exclaimed playfully. Then "Oh! this hay is pricking me awfully!"

This I soon remedied by means of my horse rug, — and then we were comfortably installed!

Outside the tempest continued to rage unabated, with loud claps of thunder and torrential rain. My pretty companion however had no alarm, and abandoned herself afresh to me. In the midst of our toyings and handlings of each others persons, I whispered: "Do take this off, — it's only a nuisance!" And I pointed first to her stays, then to her riding breeches.

"You'll do the same?"

"Yes, of course. And at once."

Gracefully she consented to satisfy my prayer, and set to work to take off her breeches, or rather her cloth knickers buttoning at the knee. When she had let them fall I helped her to draw her legs out of them and to pass them over her little patent-leather riding-boots, a task I took care not to accomplish without availing myself of the opportunity to effect sundry little ticklings and indiscreet touchings which provoked from her little screams of laughter.

"I'm going to keep on my hat," she said, "for my hair is damp and I would never be able to get it into order again!"

Oh! how bewitching she then looked! — and what a piquant costume! She stood in her chemise with her silk riding hat on, and her patent-leather riding boots halfway up her calf, the rest of her leg being covered with a grey silk stocking fastened above the knee with a rose coloured garter!

I dropped on my knees in front of her and pressed my lips upon a forest of golden hairs through which I tried to insert my tongue . . .

"No, no," she exclaimed, drawing herself back a little, — "not standing upright!" Then she lay herself down, — and pleasure invaded the pair of us!

Her chemise I had turned back and the whole of her lovely body was now exposed! I showered kisses all over it, but especially all about her thighs, between which I then recommenced my sweet occupation in a less unfavourable posture than before. My skilful tongue soon sent out of herself! — her stomach heaved agitatedly, then jogged itself spasmodically upwards as if loth to lose a single touch of my tongue!

Pleasure communicated demands reciprocity! This was always our rule and practice in the days when she was taking lessons from me in the Art and Practice of Love. Without arresting my ministrations, I placed myself in a position that I knew would recall to her our old conventions! Her soft hand showed me that she understood, as it gently seized the object I had placed at her disposal; I then brought myself still nearer, so that her mouth had even less distance than before to travel in order to carry out its sweet duty.

"No, no! that won't do!" she softly exclaimed, — "you will disarrange my hair! Let me come on top of you!" — and she gently freed herself in order to do so.

She took my place, put herself on top of me, turned without hesitation her lovely bottom towards my face, — and then lowered herself till her delicious slit rested on my mouth! And immediately I felt my member kissed, caressed, — handled, — then sucked in the most delightful fashion, I responding by furiously thrusting my tongue as deeply as I could into her throbbing quivering cunt!

The storm, the hunt, — all were completely forgotten! What ecstacies we were revelling in! . . . what delirious transports! . . . what zest she was putting in her suction of me! My lessons had borne wonderful fruit! . . . And I, with what fury I thrust my tongue into the grotto of love that was palpitating on my lips! . . . how I licked, sucked, nibbled! . . . But I began to feel I was . . .

"Diana! . . . Diana! . . . stop! . . . stop! . . . I'm coming! . . . coming!"

Alas! — too late! A suction more subtle and overpowering than anything that had preceded it deprived me of the power of moving! — and my boiling discharge shot into the sweet mouth of my companion!

Shocked by such a catastrophe, I feared a legitimate punishment. But nothing happened! To cover my fault, I continued to pass my tongue into and over Mme de Schoenfutz's cunt till she lay motionless! Perhaps my now somewhat calmed ardour was expressed by my tongue! Perhaps my lovely companion herself had spent deliciously! Presently I began to make my apologies.

"My sweet Diana, really I beg pardon . . ."

She made no reply, — but raised herself off me, rosy red, approached me as if to kiss me, — put her lips on mine . . . and spat into my mouth the liqueur she had been storing so carefully in hers! Then shaking with laughter she remarked wickedly, "There, you've got it all back!"

Delighted by so happy a solution, I caught hold of her, captured her bottom, raised her chemise, and set to work to slap her playfully, but not for long — for I bent down and covered her charming hemispheres with numberless kisses.

Before long, thanks to a thousand erotic

follies, the standard-bearer of my desires — the "Leader of the shocking party" (as a witty English girl once called it) became again rampant and erect. This time we gave the preference to a sacrifice to Venus in the ordinary method; for however delicious may be other postures and the other ways of performing the act of fucking, they are more or less *hors-d'oeuvres*, tit-bits, rather than a substantial meal. — But owing to her hat my partner took the upper place, — and very soon, clasped in each others arms, lips against lips, my prick penetrated into the sweet opening already lubricated by my kisses and tongueings!

Just then the rain came down with an intensity hitherto unequalled, as so often happens towards the end of a storm. Mme de Schoenfutz began to squirm and wriggle in a most extraordinary way, — it was with the greatest difficulty that I managed to keep her impaled on my prick in spite of my hands being firmly pressed on the two charming rotundities which women so love to exaggerate in their toilettes.

"The rain is coming through," she explained, I can feel some drops just in the small of my back. Oh! there's one!

"Shall we change places?"

"No! . . . No! . . . oh! there's another, just between the cheeks of my bottom! Oh! how it tickles!" And again she squirmed and wriggled in the most voluptuous way as she lay on me!

The rain was really coming through the roof. But what did we care! The blissful ecstatic crisis was approaching! — our breath mixed with our humid lips! — I began to feel that I could not hold back my boiling discharge for long! Among our mutual understandings, it was decreed that I was not to deposit my tribute of love inside the shrine (whichever it might be) into which I had been permitted to perform my worship. My recent infraction was one which would carry no grave after-consequences, — it was only perhaps an offence to shame; but if I now should repeat it the result might be most serious and in fact might damage Mme de Schoenfutz's reputation! So I murmured in her ear softly that I was getting to the end of my powers of self-control, that I must soon . . . spend! . . . that something was just . . . coming! and that I must withdraw my prick while I was sufficiently master of myself to do so!

"Wait! . . . wait! . . . one moment! . . . I'm . . . finishing . . . also! . . ." she gasped brokenly as her movements on me accelerated, accompanied by convulsions of pleasure! . . . A few ecstatic thrills, and then the sudden relaxing of her body announced that her blissful crisis had come and gone! — that she had spent! . . . Then promptly I withdrew my prick out of its sweet nook and . . . discharged! . . . not wasting my ammunition however, as I slipped my rampant prick between the quivering globes of her bottom and inundated the charming valley that lay between them with a deluge of another sort to what had come from the roof!

"Oh! . . . oh! . . ." she ejaculated, "it has reached right up to my back! . . . it's much warmer than the rain!"

* * * *

After we had crept down again, we found our garments quite dry. I helped my companion to dress.

"Is my hair much tumbled? I expect you've rumpled it horribly!"

"No, not at all. It's all right." And I kissed her tenderly.

She drew out of her pocket a little powder box and passed the puff lightly over her face.

"You Viennese ladies are very fond of rice powder!" I said.

"O yes. I use it all over me!"

"Don't I know it?" I replied maliciously.

"Oh! you wretch!"

We remounted our horses. The rain had ceased; the forest was full of the delightful fragrance which leaves give out after a shower.

Our road back took us close to a keeper's

house where we made enquiries about the hunting and were told that it had not been recommenced. Just then a group of horsemen came from T... where they had taken shelter; among them was M. de Z... We joined them.

"So you took refuge here?" he enquired of me.

"No, not I, Mme de Schoenfutz did. I came by just as she was remounting. I stopped with the keeper, Jean."

\* \* \* \*

In the drawing-room the same evening, the conversation turned on the storm and the interrupted hunt, and everyone told how he or she had fared while sheltering.

"In the house I was in," said Mme de Schoenfutz, "they made me taste a sort of white sauce . . . You know it!" she added looking at me!

"Oh, yes!" I stammered, staggered by her audacity, — "as I was passing you called me in!"

"Yes, that was so, and I made you try it, but you did not seem to fancy it!"

Her coolness simply dumbfounded me!

Then they all began to discuss what it could have been; every one expressed some opinion, but an old maid insisted that she knew it.

"Of course it was only milk thickened with

maize powder! When it is warm and not too thick, it is very nice!!"

# PART II

I was fifteen years old when my mother was seized with an illness which proved to be fatal. After eight months of suffering, she left this life. Realizing the depth of my sorrow at the loss, my father cherished me all the more, and I returned his tenderness with all my heart.

I was continually the object of his caresses. Not a day passed without his cuddling me and covering my face and lips with the most passionate kisses.

I remember that my mother had reproached him one day for the liberties he was taking with my body.

'What are you complaining about, Madame?' he had replied. 'I am doing nothing wrong. If she were my daughter, the censure would be justified. I am no Lot.'

This incident never left my memory, although I did not understand until some time later. I clung to him, however, since I knew I owed everything to him. It was not hard to do, for he was the soul of affection and solicitude.

So favoured was I by nature that he believed that the deity of love had fashioned me. He never tired of telling that to me. From my infancy, I showed promise of a pleasing, svelte figure and a face with regular features. The vivacity of my brown eyes was tempered by the sweetness of my glance. Although I was lively and gay, I had a tendency to be reflective.

My father studied carefully my tastes and inclinations, which he cultivated and developed with the greatest diligence. One thing that he was insistent on was that I hold nothing back from him. It was a condition I found no difficulty in meeting. His tenderness for me was such that on the infrequent occasions when he thought I deserved to be punished, the blows were caresses.

Some time after the death of my mother, he took me in his arms.

'Laurette, my dear child,' he said, 'It is now time to think of your education.'

With my father as my sole teacher, I received the most brilliant training imaginable. He was familiar with everything – drawing, dancing, music, literature and the sciences.

Although my father was occupied with my upbringing, I noticed him often sunk deep in thought and perturbed. It was obvious that something was bothering him. After my mother's demise, we had left our home in the country to live in the city. Since he had few other interests, I became the centre of his life and the object of all his affection.

The caresses he lavished on me seemed to animate him, for his eyes sparkled, his face turned red, and his lips became dry and hot. He liked to take my buttocks in his hands and massage them. Or he passed a finger over my thighs while he kissed my mouth and breast. Often, he completely undressed me and lowered my naked body into a bath. After having dried me and rubbed oils and essences into my skin, he put his lips to every part of my body excepting one. As he contemplated me, he shook all over. Then his hands were again on me. How I liked this delightful game. Then suddenly he ceased his fiery manipulations to run and lock himself in his study.

One day, when his kisses were more impassioned than usual, kisses I returned with my usual tenderness, and our mouths were glued together with his tongue moistening my lips, I suddenly felt strange sensations. The flame of his embraces had slipped into my veins. He then escaped me when I least expected it and great was my chagrin. Also, I was curious to learn what had attracted him to his room, but when I tried to open the door, I found it latched.

The following day, he was given a letter which seemed to please him. After having read it a second time, he spoke to me.

'My dear Laura, it is time for you to have a governess. One is arriving tomorrow. Although she comes with the highest recommendations, I have to see her for myself to make my own judgment if they are exaggerated or not.'

I was totally unprepared for such news which, for some reason, greatly saddened me. Without knowing why, I was uncomfortable at her presence and I did not like her even before I had seen her.

Lucette arrived the day before she was expected. She was a big girl around nineteen or twenty with an opulent bosom, extremely white skin, a good but not unusual figure, a pretty mouth with carmine lips, and two perfect rows of enamel teeth. Immediately my preconception of her was changed. In addition, she had an excellent character, an abundance of gentleness and kindness, and a winning way. I was completely taken by her, and we soon became the most intimate friends. It was evident that my father was more than satisfied with her.

Envy and jealousy are strangers to my soul. Besides, what arouses the desire of men often is not our beauty or our merit. Thus, for the sake of our own happiness, it is wisest to let them alone and not to worry. More often than not their infidelity is nothing more than a slight fire that goes out as soon as it is lit. Consequently, it is folly to torment oneself about it.

Although I was not yet capable of reasoning in such a way at that time, I still felt no animosity towards Lucette. Besides, there was no diminishment in the signs of affection that my father bestowed on me. The only thing I perceived was his reserve when she was present but I put this down to mere shyness. Some weeks passed in this fashion until I finally noticed the attentions he was paying her. He never let an opportunity escape to reveal his feelings towards her. It was not long before I shared his sentiments for her.

When Lucette expressed her desire to sleep in my room, my father readily gave his consent. When he awoke in the morning, the first thing he did was to enter our chamber in which our beds were side to side. This arrangement enabled him to make advances towards Lucette while pretending that he had come to see me.

It was obvious that she was not rebuffing him, but she did not respond to his urgings as quickly as I would have liked her to, and I could not figure out the reason for her dragging feet. Loving my father as much as I did, I was of the opinion that everybody should feel towards him as I did. I could not help but chide her for her indifference.

'Why don't you like my Papa?' I asked her one day. 'He seems to have such warm feelings for you. I think that you are very ungrateful.'

She merely smiled at these reproaches, assuring me that I was doing her an injustice. She was right, for in a short time the apparent coolness vanished.

One evening after supper, we retired to a salon where my father had coffee and liqueurs served. In less than half an hour, Lucette was sound asleep. At that, my father took me up in his arms and carried me to my room where he put me to bed. Surprised at this new arrangement, my curiosity was instantly aroused. I got up a few moments later and tip-toed to the glass door, whose velvet curtain I slightly pushed aside so that I could look into the salon.

I was astonished to see Lucette's bosom completely uncovered. What charming breasts she possessed! They were two hemispheres as white as snow and firm as marble in the centre of which rose two little strawberries. The only movement they showed was from her regular breathing. My father was fondling them, kissing them and sucking them. In spite of his actions, she continued slumbering. Soon he began to remove all of her clothing, placing it on the edge of the bed. When he took off her shift, I saw two plump, rounded thighs of alabaster which he spread apart.

Then I made out a little vermilion slit adorned with a chestnut-brown tuft of hair. This he half opened, inserting his fingers which he vigorously manipulated in and out. Nothing roused her out of her lethargy.

Excited by the sight and instructed by the example, I imitated on myself the movements I saw and experienced sensations hitherto unknown to me. Laying her on the bed, my father came to the glass door to close it. I saved myself by hastening to the couch on which he had placed me. As soon as I was stretched out on the sheets, I began my rubbing, pondering what I had just viewed and profiting from what I had learned. I was on fire. The sensation I was undergoing increased in intensity, reaching such a height that it seemed my entire body and soul were concentrated in that one spot. Finally, I sank back in a state of exhausted ecstasy that enchanted me.

Returning to my senses, I was astonished to find myself almost soaked between my thighs. At first, I was very worried, but this anxiety was dispelled by the remembrance of the bliss I had just enjoyed. I fell into a deep sleep filled with dreams of my father caressing me. I was not yet awake when he came the next morning to awaken me with kisses which I eagerly returned.

Since that day, my governess and he seemed to have a secret understanding, although in the morning he did not remain with us as he formerly did. Of course, they had not the slightest suspicion that I was *au courant* as to what was going on, and lulled into a false security, during the day, they shamelessly flirted before retiring to my father's room where they remained for long periods of time.

With justice, I imagined that they were going to repeat what I had already seen, and my ideas did not go any further than that. Nevertheless, I was dying to view the same spectacle again. The reader can picture to himself the violent desire that was tormenting me. Finally came the moment when I was to learn everything.

Three days after the event I have just described, I took advantage of my father's absence to satisfy my burning curiosity. While Lucette was engaged in some task in another part of the house, I punctured a little hole in the silken curtain of the glass door.

I had not long to wait to profit from my stratagem.

On my father's return, he immediately donned a flimsy dressing-gown and led to his room Lucette, who was in equally casual attire. They were careful to close the door and draw the curtain, but my preparations frustrated their precautions, at least in part. As soon as they were in the room, I was at the door with my face glued to the glass by the lifted curtain. The first person to meet my eyes was Lucette with her magnificent bosom completely bare. It was so seductive that I could not blame my father for immediately covering it with quick, eager kisses. Unable to hold himself back he tore off her clothing, and in a twinkling of the eye, skirt, corset and chemise were on the floor. How temptingly lovely she was in her natural state! I could not tear my eyes from her. She possessed all the charms and freshness of youth. Feminine beauty has a singular power and attraction for those of the same sex. My arms yearned to embrace those divine contours.

My father was soon in a state similar to his partner's. My eyes were fixed on him, because I had never seen him that way before. Now he placed her on the divan, which I could not see from my observation post.

Devoured by curiosity, I threw caution to the winds. I lifted the curtain until I could see everything. Not a detail escaped my eyes, and they spared themselves not the slightest voluptuousness.

I was able to perceive clearly Lucette stretched out on the couch and her fully expanded slit between the two chubby eminences. My father displayed a veritable jewel, a big member, stiff, surrounded by hair at the root below which dangled two balls. The tip was a scarlet red. I saw it enter Lucette's slit, lose itself there, and then reappear. This in-and-out movement continued for some time. From the fiery kisses they exchanged, I surmised that they were in raptures. Finally, I noticed the organ completely emerge. From the carmine tip which was all wet spurted a white fluid on Lucette's flat belly.

How the sight aroused me! I was so excited and carried away by desires I had not yet known that I attempted, at least partially, to participate in their delirium.

So entranced was I by the tableau that I remained too long and my imprudence betrayed me. My father, who had been too preoccupied with Lucette, now, disengaging himself from Lucette's arms, saw the partially lifted curtain. On spotting me, he wrapped himself in his robe as he approached the door. I hastily withdrew, but he raised the drape and discovered me trying to beat a retreat.

He stationed himself at the door while Lucette was

dressing. Seeing that he remained motionless, I fancied that he had not noticed anything. Still curious to know what was going on, I returned to the curtain. My astonishment when I met his face on the other side can be imagined. I was thunderstruck with fright.

By this time, Lucette had her clothes back on. My father pretended that nothing was amiss. Reminding Lucette of certain errands she had to carry out, he dismissed her, and I was alone with him.

When he came up to me, I was trembling and pale with fear. But, to my great surprise, instead of castigating me, he took me in his arms and covered me with a hundred kisses.

'Calm yourself, my dear Laurette,' he comforted me. 'Who in the world could have inspired the terror I see in your eyes? You need have no fear, my darling. You know that I have never harmed you. All I ask of you now is the truth. At this moment, I want you to consider me a friend rather than your father. Laura, I am your friend, and I beseech you to be sincere with me. Don't conceal anything from me. Tell me what you were doing when I was with Lucette and the reason for your peeking around this curtain. If you are honest, you will not have any reason to repent. If you aren't, my warm feelings for you will vanish and you can count on the convent.'

The mere mention of the final word had always filled me with dread. What I had heard of the life in those retreats! I mentally contrasted life there to that with my father. Besides, I had no doubt that I had witnessed everything. Finally, from past experience, I knew the wisdom of avowing everything to him, and I blurted out the entire truth.

Each detail I told him and each tableau I retraced, far from igniting his wrath, was repaid with kisses and caresses. I hesitated, nevertheless, at confessing the new, delicious experiences I had procured by myself, but he suspected them.

'Darling Laurette, you still haven't told me all,' he remarked, as he passed his hands over my derriere and kissed me. 'You should not hide anything from me. Give me the whole story.'

With some reluctance, I admitted that I had imitated his friction movements with Lucette, which had produced in me the most wonderful sensations. Even though I got all wet from doing it, I had repeated it three or four times, always with the same pleasure.

'But, dear Laura,' he cried, 'seeing what I put into Lucette, didn't you get the idea of inserting your finger into yourself?'

'No, Papa, the thought never crossed my mind.'

'Don't try to deceive me,' he warned. 'You can't hide anything from me. Come over here so I can see if you are telling the truth.'

'Honestly, Papa, I have told you the truth,' I protested.

Using the most endearing words with me, he led me into his bedroom, where he stretched me out on a couch. He lifted up my skirt and examined me carefully. Then, slightly opening my narrow slit, he tried to penetrate it with his little finger. The screams from the pain he was causing me made him stop.

'It is all inflamed, my child. Nevertheless, I recognize that you have not lied to me. The redness undoubtedly is due to the friction you committed on yourself while I was with Lucette.'

Now that I had lost my fear, I even told him that I could not obtain the pleasure I was looking for. The sincerity of my mouth was rewarded by a kiss from his. Then he lowered it, and with his tongue, tickled a certain spot that made me squeal with delight. I found this kind of caress new and heavenly. To bring my raptures to a peak he produced that member I had seen before. Involuntarily, I took it with one hand, while with the other, I opened his robe. He made no objection. I regarded with admiration and fondled that joyous instrument that I had seen disappear into Lucette's interior. How pleasing and unusual it was! From the first moment I touched it, I instinctively realized that it was the originator of pleasure. It went up and down in rhythm with the movement of my hand, which covered and uncovered the skin of the tip. Imagine my surprise when, after several moments of this sport, I saw gush out the same fluid that had flooded Lucette's thighs. As the last drops oozed, I noticed that he was trembling all over. I was happy that I had given a pleasure which I partially shared.

When I released my sticky hand, he resumed his previous game with his tongue. I was dying of an ineffable bliss. I was suffocating, but he continued.

'Dear Papa, stop it!' I pleaded. 'I can't stand it any longer.'

I fainted in his arms.

From that time on, everything became clear to me. What I had guessed before became a certainty. It seemed that the instrument I was touching was the magic key to understanding. Because of that organ, my father became even dearer to me. And my sentiments for him were returned in like measure.

He led me back to my room, where my governess appeared a few moments later. I did not have the slightest idea of what he was about to say to her.

'Lucette, from now on it is senseless to watch our step with Laura, for she knows everything.'

Then he repeated to her everything I had related to him and showed her the curtain. She appeared very disturbed, but I threw my arms around her neck, and my embraces, along with the reasons I gave her, quickly dissipated the embarrassment she had evinced. Kissing us both, he told Lucette not to leave me out of her sight. He left, returning an hour later with a woman who, as soon as she was in the room, made me completely disrobe and took my measurements for a sort of garment, the form of use of which I could not guess.

When it came time to go to bed, my father put me in Lucette's bed, admonishing her to keep an eye on me. Once again he departed, only to return a few minutes later and crawl in the same bed with us. I was between the two of them. My father held me in a tight hug. Covering with his hand the space between my legs, he prevented me from putting mine at that spot. I took his instrument, which surprised me because it was so limp and moist. I had never seen it in this pitiable state, imagining that it was always swollen, stiff and erect. But in my hand it was no longer slow in regaining the condition in which I knew it.

Lucette, who perceived what we were doing, was shocked.

'What you are doing with Laurette is outrageous,' she reproved him. 'Especially since you are her father.'

'You are partially right, Lucette,' he replied. 'But it is a secret that I wish to confide to you. It is to Laura's own interest that she keep her silence. Circumstances make it necessary that I tell you both.

'I had known her mother only fifteen days when I married her. The very first day after the wedding, I discovered her condition, but I considered it the wisest course to pretend not to notice it. In order that dates could not be put together, I took her to a distant province. After four months, Laura entered the world with all the vigour and health of a normal nine month infant. For six months more, I remained in that province, after which I brought the two back home. Now you recognize that this child who is so dear to me is not my own daughter in the strict sense of the word. Although she is not bound to me by flesh and blood, she is as dear to me as if she were.'

Then I immediately recalled the reply he had made to my mother's reproaches. The silence she maintained no longer appeared strange.

'But how could you have acted in such a way towards your wife?' Lucette wanted to know.

'Oh, I was never close to my wife,' my father nonchalantly answered. 'The Count de Norval, to whom Laura owes her entry into this life, is a likeable nobleman, a fine figure of a man with a handsome face, possessing those qualities that interest women. I wasn't the least bit surprised to learn that my wife had

27

succumbed to his attack. However, she was unable to marry him, for her parents did not find him wealthy enough for her. But if Laura is not my daughter by blood, the affection I have conceived for this adorable child renders her perhaps even more dear to me.

'Nevertheless, because of the mother's falsity I never approached her. I had an antipathy for her that I could not overcome. That is why I turned all my love to the innocent child.'

Lucette lavished on me hugs and kisses which told me that all her prejudices had been effaced. Warmly I returned her tokens of affection, even taking her enticing breasts and kissing and sucking the pink tips. My father stretched his hand to her and met mine, which he passed over Lucette's stomach and her thighs. Now my hand was guided over the fleece, the *mons Veneris*, and the crevice. I soon learned the names of all these portions of the female anatomy. Then I put my finger on the spot where I thought I would cause her pleasure. There I came across something rather hard and distended.

'Good, Laura!' my father complimented me. 'You are holding the most sensitive part. Move your hand without relinquishing the clitoris while I stick my finger in her little cunt.'

Lucette, her arm about me, caressing my buttocks, took my father's prick and introduced it between my thighs, but he did not put it in nor did he make the slightest movement. Soon my governess was at the peak of pleasure. Her kisses multiplied and her sighs became moans.

'Stop! That's enough!' she moaned. 'Faster! Put it

in all the way, my dearest. My God, I am coming! This is the end.'

How these expressions of voluptuousness delighted me. I felt that her cunt was all damp. My father's finger came out, all covered with what she had discharged. I was beside myself with excitement. Taking Lucette's hand, I brought it to between my legs so that she would do to me what I had done for her, but my father, covering my mound with his hand, stopped her. He was too much of a libertine not to be sparing of his pleasures, and he moderated his desires, leaving me up in the air by recommending us to calm ourselves. We fell asleep, our arms interlaced, plunged into the sweetest intoxication. I had never spent such a delicious night.

When the rays of the morning sun brought us back to life, Lucette and I looked at each other. Then I noticed a note pinned to the chair. It was from Papa who wrote that he would be away all day, but he knew that Lucette would take good care of me. Excitedly, I reminded my companion that it was the servants' day off and we would be alone. We beamed at each other with radiant smiles.

I nestled closer to her for I loved to sniff the sharp odour that came from her svelte body. I nuzzled my nose between her breasts to breathe it in more deeply. It reminded me of carrots, and every time I smelled it, I quivered with excitement.

'I think I am too fat,' she remarked. 'Don't you think so?'

She lifted up her nightgown as if to prove her point. I wondered why she thought she was so fat. Her legs were lovely and well-rounded, and her buttocks dimpled and charming. There was not the trace of a bulge on her body. The magnificent breasts were so heavy that I wondered how they could jut out as they did. And I could not keep my eyes from the clump of luxuriant hair under her armpits. When she turned her back to me, I saw her derriere, two superb hemispheres that must have been fashioned in heaven.

'You are not too plump,' I affirmed again. 'On the contrary, it seems to me that you are just right.'

She gave me a pleased pout as she got out of bed and walked to the desk with the cheeks of her bottom swaying seductively from side to side. She returned to the warm bed with a large album of art reproductions, many of them of nude women and in col ur.

'Look,' she said, pointing out one to me. 'She is far more slender than I.'

'Yes, but on the other hand, this woman by Rubens is far plumper than you.'

'That may be so, but I still should lose some weight. A massage does the trick, and you can help me if you wish.'

'I? . . . Massage you? I have never done that before. . . .'

'There's nothing difficult about it. It's just the sort of favour one does for a friend. And you are my friend, aren't you?'

I puffed up with pride at that. But I felt a certain uneasiness not unmingled with anticipation.

'And I have just the thing for a massage,' she added with a slight blush.

'What do you mean by that?' I asked her in some puzzlement. 'I always thought you massaged with the hands.'

'There are also appliances that are helpful in removing excess flesh. . . . I'll get mine.'

She went to her room and came back with a rubber glove covered with bumps. It reminded me of the skin of a toad. Lucette ran it up and down my arm. It gave me goose-pimples but the sensation was not unpleasant.

'How do you like it, Laura?' she asked with a glint in her eyes.

Then she applied it on her shoulders, her arms and above her breasts. I felt a twinge of envy.

'I hope I'll be able to use it correctly and not hurt you. I have never seen anything like that before. If I am clumsy, please forgive me.'

'There's no danger, but I'll have to lie down.'

Now she was on her stomach, lovelier than ever, particularly since her lush body was reflected in the wall mirror.

'Now start at the top of my back,' she ordered.

This promised to be fun. The skin quivered and turned pink where I touched it with my gloved hand. Lucette remained motionless, her head between her arms and her hair over her ears. After vigorously treating the glorious buttocks, she suddenly turned over.

'And now the breasts, Laura.'

Nervously, I did as I was bid. The gorgeous globes shivered as much as my hand. Taking my hand, she made it descend to one of the rosy nipples.

'Look,' she said.

To my astonishment, I saw it dilate, swell, get hard and jut out. It became a crimson mountain peak. Then she made me put it on the other. As I rubbed

31

the mound, there occurred, to my uneasiness, the same phenomenon.

'I'm in heaven,' Lucette blissfully sighed. 'That's the way nipples become when they are handled that way. Now the belly, Laura, and the hips. It is so wonderful when you do it, and I can't tell you how grateful I am.'

My eyes were glued to the hard breasts, the hollow navel, and the dark triangle whose hair extended almost all the way up to her waist. Mentally, I compared myself with her. I had only a pitiful little fleece there, while hers was a carpet, a beautiful luxurious Persian rug.

I revolved the glove on her stomach around her navel. I did not dare get too close to the triangle, for I was afraid that it might get tangled in the matted hair and hurt her. She was lasciviously wiggling her hips with her eyes shut. It was obvious that she was in an incipient ecstasy. Her toes contracted and sometimes her knee twitched when I got too close to the erogenous zone.

'Now between the thighs,' she murmured without opening her eyes. I observed that her nipples were straining more than ever.

Reassured that I was giving her pleasure, I redoubled my efforts as I rubbed the glove on the silky skin. But I could not keep my eyes from the luxuriant thicket. I wondered how what it was concealing would look like.

I was sure that mine would be put to shame in comparison.

The more I kept at it, the more pleasure it gave me. I was not a little disappointed when she told me to stop. Reading my feelings in my face, Lucette laughed.

'I can see that you are unwilling to give up, dearest Laura,' she said. 'But don't be disappointed, I need a bit of a breathing spell, for that puts my nerves on edge. Why, you are perspiring! Take off your nightgown. You'll be much more comfortable. I don't think you are bashful after last night.'

'A little,' I confessed, but I followed her suggestion.

'Completely nude, that's the way I want you,' she breathed. 'I adore nudity. I can never get enough of looking at myself naked in a mirror. I never feel alone when I can regard my reflection in the mirror. We were so excited last night that I did not notice what adorable little breasts you have. And what promise your delicate figure shows!'

The compliments gave me so much pleasure that I could not conceal my blushes. I wanted to bury my face in her arms. Hurling myself at her, I feverishly kissed her cheeks. She looked at me straight in the eyes, holding my gloved hands in hers.

'Continue,' she commanded.

Eagerly, too eagerly I resumed my task. She promptly rebuked me.

'Not so fast and not so hard,' she scolded. 'Just run it gently over my whole body. Do you understand?'

Now I did not press down so hard. Lucette closed her eyes in contentment.

'It's like a lover's caress,' she murmured.

In the mirror I could see the bed, the naked body of my new friend, and mine which was trembling and twitching. At the same time, I regarded my little, rounded, apple-like breasts with their tawny tips, and

33

came to the conclusion that I was not too bad. Perhaps I was not as abundant as Lucette, but I was not her inferior. My charms were just on a smaller scale.

Now her mouth was agape and her breathing laboured. I twisted the glove on her stomach and breasts. Each time I touched a nipple, she gave a start, convulsively lifted a knee, and spread her legs. When I took the rubber glove away, she became motionless.

'Farther down, Laura,' she whispered as if I were neglecting her spread thighs. I massaged the inside of them. From the knees, the glove gradually ascended to the groin and the buttocks.

It was then that I noticed a curious movement of her pelvis. She kept lifting and dropping it in fits and starts. At the same time, she was rattling in her throat and trying to catch her breath.

Going up still farther, I put the glove on the hairs of her mound. Her jerky movements became more agitated and vehement. Suddenly, she grasped my hand and spread her legs as far apart as she could.

'There . . . there!' she panted. 'Don't take it away. Keep it where it is. How good it feels!'

I was a little afraid at the way she was flopping about. Her legs shot up in the air and then limply dropped. I watched her face. It was livid, contorted in a grimace that deformed her features. Horrified, I tried to take away the glove, but she held it firmly in position. I wondered what was wrong with her. After more convulsions, both her body and face relaxed. For several minutes she remained without life or movement.

When I took off the glove, wondering if I had hurt her with it, she opened her eyes and smiled sweetly at me.

'It was sheer bliss,' she said dreamily.

I was dumbfounded. How could she say a thing like that when I had seen how she was suffering?

'You don't understand, I see,' she told me. 'And I can't explain. It is something that you have to experience yourself. Do you want me to massage you in turn?'

'But won't it hurt?' I timidly asked. 'You were groaning and moaning so, and the words you said, I was really afraid.'

'Do you love me that much, Laura?'

'Yes, yes, I love you . . . more than anything.'

In such gambols we spent the day and night.

When Lucette and I awoke, we were still locked in each other's arms. My father entered, bringing with him the woman who had come the previous day. My surprise and chagrin were great when she put on me morocco leather shorts which descended from my hips to slightly above my knees. They were loosely fitting and not constraining at all. The girdle fitted me perfectly around the waist and two straps holding up the shorts passed over my shoulders. They could be loosened or tightened at will. The girdle had an opening in the front that extended four inches down. Along this aperture, there were eyelets on both sides through which my father passed a little chain of delicately worked silver gilt which he locked with a little key.

'My dear Laura, adorable child, I am greatly concerned about your health and your preservation.

35

Chance has instructed you already in that which should only have · learned at the age of eighteen. Consequently, I have to take precautions against your premature knowledge and the inclinations you have by nature and love. In time, you'll come to share my judgment, but nothing you will say now will change my mind.'

At first I was infuriated, and I could not conceal my ill temper, but on reflection I realized the gratitude I owed my father.

He had foreseen everything. At the bottom of these shorts was a little silver gondola the size of the space between my thighs. In this my little mound was completely encased, while on either side it covered my little cunt and my asshole. It was not uncomfortable. It was so fashioned that I could perform my natural functions without any inconvenience, but it was impossible to insert my finger into the narrow aperture to masturbate, which was what my father desired to prevent above all things.

Since that time, I have often seen such contraptions on boys to keep them from wasting their virility before their time, for no matter how one keeps an eye on them, they go their own awkward way, much to their regret in later years.

For two years, my father removed the shorts every evening, which Lucette cleaned after washing me. After ascertaining that the chastity contrivance was not hurting me, he put it back on. From that day until I was eighteen, I had to wear the thing night and day. But during that period I learned a great deal, for I was curious by nature. Each year saw my knowledge increase, and I was indefatigable in my studies.

I had become used to my imprisonment, and the thought that one day I would be rid of it made it bearable.

Among the questions I most frequently asked him was the reason for my restraint and what were the precautions he was taking with regard to me, for he kept postponing my freedom until I was older. It was on my eighteenth birthday that he finally satisfied my curiosity.

'Now I think it is about time, dear Papa, for you to tell my why I have to wear this horrible thing, especially since you keep telling me how much you love me. Lucette is happier than I, and surely you care for her less than you do for me. I insist on knowing why you have done this to me.'

With that, I stamped my foot and shook my curls in determination.

'I have to agree that you are no longer a child, and it is time that I should give you an explanation. With men, nature starts to manifest itself around the age of fifteen or sixteen, but it reaches its peak at seventeen or eighteen. When one diverts its operations by premature and numerous discharges, so that this development is weakened, the results are felt for the rest of one's life.

'It is the same with women. If they waste their resources at too early an age, they will die early, become enfeebled and languid, and suffer from depression. They become so thin that they fall easy prey to tuberculosis. As a result, they are not able to enjoy the sweetest pleasure life has to offer.

'Because of my deep and tender love for you, dearest Laurette, I wanted to keep you from such a terrible fate, and what I did to you was for your own good.'

Although I had a deep-seated penchant for pleasure and voluptuousness, I had no desire to obtain them at such a price, and the prospect, as painted by my father, frightened me.

'I recognized such inclinations in you,' my father continued, 'and I knew that reason would have no power against your innate sensuousness. That is why I wanted to protect you against yourself, and I have to tell you that it is not yet time to set you free, for there are still many dangers lurking which you cannot cope with now.'

The thought of impaired health and the fear of an early death were vivid in my imagination. Nevertheless, what I had seen him do with Lucette and the way he lived with her weakened somewhat the impact of his dire predictions. I could not help but express to him my doubts.

'Why don't you take the same precautions with Lucette as you do with me, Papa? Why do you give her so often what you absolutely forbid me?'

'Why, my daughter,' he replied, 'Lucette is a fully formed woman. Besides, if she retains within her too much fluid of life, it would ravage her health by stagnating. Moreover, it would hinder the circulation of her blood. When that happens, a woman becomes dizzy, demented, exhausted and delirious. You can see horrible examples in certain nunneries where the sisters are so closely watched that they have no outlets for their natural desires. Remedies have been attempted, but the results have been worse than the cure.

'With some women, the ardour of temperament is quenched earlier than with others, and I want yours to continue as long as possible. When the time is right, you will have no cause to repent of your long continence and you will receive the life-giving fluid as copiously as Lucette does. Now you can understand my behaviour towards you.'

'Papa, for that is how I shall always call you,' I protested, 'I can understand your reasoning, but how long do I have to wait until you do with me what you do with her? I can hardly wait for that moment, since I am so eager to satisfy your desires to the fullest extent.'

'Wait until nature speaks more loudly,' he counselled me. 'Wait just a little longer when you will have the force. Then, Laurette, I shall receive the full measure of tenderness you have for me. You will allow me to pluck that rare blossom that I have been so carefully cultivating, but that moment has not yet come.'

His words were etched in my memory, and his reasoning seemed based on such a sound foundation, his readiness to answer my questions openly prompted me to query him further. I had always wondered about Lucette, who was in such a profound sleep the first time I found them together. To me, it was a mystery that I wanted cleared up. Finally, one day, I asked him.

'Papa, why was Lucette sleeping so soundly the first day you bared her breasts and why didn't she wake up while you were doing everything you wanted with her? Was she really asleep or was she just pretending?'

'She was really asleep,' he replied. 'It is a secret, but I am going to let you in on it, for it will be a lesson to you. I'll admit that for some time I was torn with desire. I became excited with you, but you could afford me no satisfaction. I liked Lucette at first sight, and I found her agreeable in every way. But seeing that she was hesitant about giving in to me, I determined on a bold step. I put some sleeping powder in the glass of liqueur that I offered her. You saw the effect. But I was not satisfied with that. I was afraid that if she woke up, surprise and anger would ruin all my plans. In order to prevent that, I had prepared in advance a potion designed to arouse all her sensuousness. That is what is called a love philtre. After I had put you in my bed, I went back to get several drops which I rubbed on her mound, her clitoris and her lips. This liquid has the power to excite even the most enfeebled and give him an erection if he smears it on his organ shortly before he enters combat.

'Lucette had not been asleep an hour before she awoke, feeling an itching, a burning, and a passion which nothing could extinguish. She did not seem surprised to see me in her arms, for she passed hers around my neck. Far from opposing my caresses and desires, for she herself was deeply moved, she voluntarily spread her legs wide. It was a matter of seconds before I was revelling in the most exquisite delights that I made her share. I was attentive to the consequences that could ensue, for at the moment when I sensed rapture ready to shoot out like a flame, I withdrew, inundating her mound and belly with a copious libation, an offering to the altar at which I was then worshipping.

'From that time, Lucette has always lent herself to my desires. It was because of her complacency, my inattention, and the curiosity I did not suspect in one your age that you discovered our secret. She does not know what I have just taught you, and you must keep my confidence.'

'You need have no worry on that score, dear Papa,' I assured him. 'But please finish your story. Aren't you afraid of getting her with child if you don't always pull out in time? Are you always in control of yourself? Aren't you sometimes carried away by ecstasy? And the fear that one has for the consequences, doesn't that diminish the pleasure?'

'Ah, my dear child,' he sighed, 'where your imagination doesn't take you! I recognize fully that I should not conceal anything from you. I don't run any risk with you, for you are intelligent beyond your years.'

'First of all, semen which is not shot into the matrix bears no fruit. There are ways to prevent it from reaching its goal, but you will learn about this when you are older. I use an infallible method with Lucette which enables her to give herself up to her passions without any worry. Before we start our lovemaking, she fits herself out with a special device which makes it impossible for her to produce children.'

I nodded in understanding.

Such were some of the conversations we had, mostly for my benefit. It goes without saying that they were frequently interrupted by kisses and caresses. Libertine books of all kinds were freely placed in my hands for me to peruse, but those that pertained to my sex

41

were stressed. We discussed religion, and according to my father, God is 'incomprehensible; he is felt rather than known. He demands our respect and despises our speculations.' My father reduced morality to, 'Do unto others as you would have them do unto you,' or 'Do not do unto others what you would not have them do unto you.'

As I pursued these studies, my figure was filling out; my pointed breasts had acquired an admirable amplitude. Every day I showed their progress to Lucette and my father, who gladly kissed them at my request. I put their hands on them to show them how firm and full they were. Finally, I made no secret of the fact that I was at the end of my patience. Never having had to curb my temper, I no longer listened to or followed anything but the voice of nature. I could see that this banter was arousing my father.

'You're getting an erection, dear Papa. Come over here,' I ordered, and placed him in Lucette's arms.

Although I was deeply aroused, I still found enjoyment in their pleasures. She and I lived in the closest intimacy; she cherished me as much as I loved her. I slept ordinarily with her, and I never failed her when my father was absent. I fulfilled my role the best I could. While hugging her, I sucked her lips and the buttons of her Junoesque breasts, and I kissed the cheeks of her derriere and her smooth belly and her delicious *mons Veneris*. I stroked her entire body. Often my fingers took the place that I could not supply her with, and I plunged her into agonies of rapture which was a delight to see. My good will and complaisance caused her to feel for me an affection that is impossible to describe. During our lovemaking, many times she had noticed me violently animated and she assured me that she ardently desired to procure for me the same ecstasies I was giving her.

'Yes, my dear Laura,' she breathed, 'when the great moment arrives, I plan on having a grand celebration. I can't wait for it. I have the feeling that the time is not far off. Your delightful breasts are just about perfectly rounded. Your arms and legs are shapely and your mound, already covered with a soft fleece, is rising. Your pretty little cunt is now a rosy pink. In your eyes, I see that something which puts you in the ranks of womanhood. Last spring, you saw some preludes of eruptions which are going to be a fact very quickly.'

Indeed, in a short time I felt more sluggish, my head was heavy, my eyes lustreless; I had pains in my back and attacks of colic. After eight days of this, Lucette found the gondola covered with blood. My father, on seeing this, did not put it back on me, for they had foreseen this. I was told of my situation. For about a week, I remained almost in a stupor, after which I was as gay and full of health as I had been before.

My happiness at my newfound freedom was indescribable. I was beside myself with joy as I threw my arms around Lucette's neck.

'How happy I am going to be!' I cried.

Then I ran to my father, whom I likewise embraced, and exultantly told him: 'Here I am in the state in which you desire me. How happy I shall be if I can arouse your desires and satisfy them! My bliss is to belong entirely to you. My love and tenderness are the goal of my felicity.'

Taking me in his arms, he sat me on his knees. With

43

what passion he returned the embraces I bestowed on him. He squeezed and kissed my woman's breasts; he sucked my lips; his tongue sought mine; and my buttocks and my cunt were both victims of his feverish hands.

'The moment has finally come, dearest Laurette,' he panted, 'this blessed instant when your tenderness and mine are going to be united in the breast of voluptuousness. I want to have your maidenhead this very day, to pluck the flower that has just blossomed. I owe it to your love, and your sentiments towards me put an inestimable value on the offering you are about to make. But I should warn you that if ineffable bliss follows our embraces and kisses, the moment when I become master of that charming rosebud, you will be pricked by some thorns that will cause you pain.'

'What does it matter?' I exclaimed. 'Make me suffer. Slash me until I bleed if you wish. I cannot make enough sacrifices for you. Your pleasure and your satisfaction are the sole object of my desires.'

My eyes were sparkling. The ever-helpful Lucette, wishing to cooperate in the bloodletting of the victim, showed herself as eager as if she had been herself the executioner. They lifted me up and carried me into a chamber that they had prepared for the time when I would be ready. The light of day was completely banished from it. In a recess surrounded by mirrors was a bed covered with a blue satin covering, and on it was a cushion of fire-red silk which was to be the sacrificial altar.

Quickly, Lucette exposed all the charms nature had bestowed on me. I, the sacrifice, was adorned only with crimson ribbons which she knotted above my elbows and waist. I resembled another Venus. Another ribbon was woven in my loose hair. Without any hesitation, I threw myself on the couch.

Regarding myself in the mirrors, I found myself more beautiful than I would be had I been wearing any ornaments. I felt very satisfied with myself. My skin was of a dazzling whiteness; my little but firm pink nipples rose proudly from the enticing breasts; a delicate fleece shaded the plump little mound, which, slightly open, revealed a clitoris stuck out from between two lips called pleasure and voluptuousness. Add to that a svelte, shapely figure, slender legs ending in dainty feet, buttocks like little apples, and a small of the back with all the freshness of Hebe. If I had been competing against the three goddesses, Paris certainly would have bestowed the apple of victory on me. Such was the praise that Lucette and my father vied in heaping on me. I was bursting with pride. The more I thought myself lovely, the more they encouraged me in the belief. My father in particular could not get over my charms. He examined and admired me. His hands and ardent lips were all over my body. We were like two young lovers who up until now had met only with difficulty and who were going to get recompense for their patience and affection.

I so wanted to see him in the state I was. At my insistence, he quickly ripped off his clothing with the assistance of Lucette. He arranged me on the bed so that my derriere was on the cushion. In my hand I held the sacred blade that in an instant was to immolate my virginity. This prick that I was passionately

45

caressing was of a stiffness to prove to me that it would surely pierce the rose that he had so carefully tended for such a long time. My imagination was burning with desire. My cunt was on fire and calling for that dear prick which I immediately set on its path.

We were locked in each other's arms, glued to each other. Our mouths and tongues devoured one another. I noticed that he was holding himself back, but passing my legs over his rump and squeezing as hard as I could, I gave an upward thrust with my backside so that he went in as far as he could go. The pain I felt and the scream that escaped from my lips were signs of his victory.

Inserting her hand between us, Lucette stroked my cunt and with the other hand tickled my asshole. The melange of pain and pleasure, and the flowing fuck and blood raised me to paradise, to an ineffable sensuousness.

I was suffocating; I was expiring. My arms and legs became limp and my head sagged. I was no longer among the living. But I took a delectation in these excesses that I could barely stand. What an exquisite state! Soon I was roused from my sweet lethargy by renewed caresses. He kissed me, sucked me, and massaged my breasts, the cheeks of my derriere, and my mount. He lifted my legs into the air to have the pleasure of regarding from a different angle my backside, my cunt and the ravages he had committed. His prick that I was still clutching and his testicles which Lucette was stroking were soon restored to their former rigidity. The former he quickly inserted into me. Now that the passage had been made easier, his penetration was nothing but sheer joy. Goodhearted Lucette renewed her titillations, and I again fell back into the lascivious apathy I had just experienced.

My father, proud of his triumph and delighted at the willingness with which I had succumbed, took the bloodstained cushion that was under me and embraced it as the trophy of his victory.

'Dear Laura,' he said as he tenderly lay down on the pillow, 'good Lucette has multiplied your pleasures. Don't you think it would be the right thing to do to let her join in our frolics?'

I threw my arms around her neck and pulled her down with me on the bed, where I lifted up her skirt and found her all damp.

'How aroused you must have been,' I said understandingly. 'Now I wish to give you at least a portion of the bliss I have just enjoyed.'

Taking my father's hand, I introduced one finger into her and he pushed it in and out while I caressed her. It was a matter of instants before she was in that state of ecstasy from which I had just emerged.

By now, we were soaked in sweat, and Papa suggested we all take a bath together. Lucette and I enthusiastically agreed. The three of us rushed to the large tub which Papa had foresightedly filled with lukewarm water beforehand. Papa and Lucette were the first to get in and then I. Being the youngest, it was I who soaped them down. Papa complimented me on my enthusiasm for my task, which I did not find irksome in the least. I paid special attention to the opulent breasts and Junoesque derriere of my governess and the shaggy hair on the chest and at the bottom of the stomach of my supposed sire. His sex was the particular object of my care. As a joke, I inserted the bar of soap into Lucette's slit. This caused general merriment.

After I bestowed a filial kiss on Papa's virility, it was my turn to receive their attention. First smearing me from chin to knees, he started a systematic fondling to which I reacted with ardour. Then we rinsed ourselves with fresh water to get rid of the mucous irritations caused by the soap. Once we were dried, Papa felt in a jovial mood.

'Lucette, let's show little Laura some games she has not seen.'

'Oh yes, let's,' Lucette cried, clapping her hands. 'But Laura has to help.'

'Indeed she does.'

Papa sat on the bidet, which I was ordered to fill with water up to the brim. His testicles and backside were completely wetted. Then I had to sit behind him with my arms around his waist. Under Lucette's guidance, my right hand began to stroke his masculinity while the left squeezed and released the testicles. Finally, my finger was led into his rear aperture. He gave a start and squeal of joy.

Lucette went back into the bedroom and returned with two thick books which she placed before Papa's feet, one on each side of the bidet. Then she stepped on them, placing her hands on his shoulders. In this position, the matted shaggy mound, already moist with desire, was directly in front of his face. Without hesitation, he darted his tongue into the inviting grotto. For better penetration, he firmly clutched the two callipygian hemispheres of his lovely Lucette.

Releasing one of them, he dipped his finger into the vagina which he vigorously stirred.

Now the only sounds heard were the grunts of the lovers and the slipslop of Papa's tongue lapping the vulva and the clitoris to the tempo of my hands fondling his sex and swollen sacks. So that I could take part in the sport, Papa withdrew his hand from Lucette and began to titillate my excited inflamed button.

It was Papa who reached bliss first. His initial jet was so powerful that it splattered the wall and drenched Lucette's thighs. The succeeding spurts plopped into the bidet water like hail stones on a pond. The sound triggered Lucette and myself to release our fluids, which we did with long lingering sighs.

We were so exhausted that some repose was necessary. Lucette and Papa were soon dozing in the bed, while I went to my room. When I came back, I saw that they were just awakening. I hid behind the curtain. Lucette was smiling affectionately at Papa and her affectionate embraces soon produced another erection. At the sight of the angry organ, she felt overwhelming desire. With a jerk of her powerful derriere, she threw off the sheets and blankets, pressed her fleshy lips on the hirsute torso, nibbling the nipples, and slid her mouth down to the navel. One of her hands blindly clutched the pulsating virility. Getting off the bed and kneeling on the rug, she thrust her head between Papa's dangling legs.

When Papa espied me, I gave a little cry of surprise, covered my eyes with my hands, and taking off my shift, clambered into the bed with Papa. I shoved a pillow under his head and put my thighs over him. I dug my hands into his wavy hair.

Papa was unable to resist the temptation of the delicious slit, which I had slightly perfumed, right in front of his nose. As his tongue automatically thrust itself into it, I gave a shriek of delight and squeezed his head tightly between my two legs. I was beside myself with pleasure at the cadence of his tongue which I regulated with the up-and-down movement of my pelvis. I took particular joy in rubbing my irritated clitoris on his nose.

Abandoning her fellation, Lucette got up and bestrode Papa on the edge of the bed. This change of position somewhat cooled Papa's ardour, for he was on the verge of ejaculating in Lucette's mouth if only she had continued her oral activity. After several downward thrusts, she was unable to hold back her orgasm and collapsed on my shoulders, gasping with pleasure. At that, I went into an almost uncontrollable spasm and gushed my inner glycerine into Papa's mouth.

Breathless, Lucette and I fell back in a near faint. Of the three of us, Papa was the only one who felt cheated, and he demanded recompense. He nodded at Lucette, who shook her head in refusal. There was only myself left, but I could see that he was reluctant to re-enter my cunt, still tight and narrow in spite of my recent defloration. But he began to caress the labia and tickle the clitoris. He whispered a few words into Lucette's ear.

She promptly stretched out on the sheets and ordered me to get on top of her, back to belly. Then Lucette put her legs on mine, spreading her knees as far apart as she could. With this manoeuvre, she so widened my cunt that the interior gaped open. It was now child's play for Papa to insert his weapon into the still damp aperture.

I was delighted and more than ready for another bout. But still the memory of the first pain caused me worry. But like a skilled tactician, Papa launched a surprise attack. His first rhythmic thrusts were barely perceptible. It seemed that the hymen had again erected its barrier. He stopped for several seconds before starting again his methodical boring, gradually gaining a few centimetres at a time. When I relaxed, he pursued his advantage to win a little more ground. Now he was at the halfway mark with another victory in sight if he did not make a misstep.

Now he employed another method of ingress, this time a corkscrew movement. In my delirium, I could see the expression of triumph on his face when he felt that it was succeeding.

Success crowned his efforts. The fleshy sword was in to the bottom of me, in spite of the narrowness of the contested valley.

I was groaning with a pleasure I had never before experienced – the first time the pain had blunted the bliss – and marvelling at the sensation in the depths of my stomach. It was a victory that Papa could well be proud of. The look on his face seemed to say: 'Ah, my little one. I finally got you. You got me to stick my tongue in your cunt, but in turn you got a prick that is going to give you a squirt you'll never forget.'

I was conquered.

I was dripping wet inside and it eased the action of his piston. Now he went at his work in a rage. His belly slapped the victim's with every jab. Sensing the approach of the supreme moment, Lucette released my lips and inserted her finger to Papa's slimy rear hole.

The reaction was immediate. In a roar of triumph and voluptuousness, Papa stopped his frenzied injections and stiffened as he shot the hot jets of his sperm into the ecstatic womb which answered his stream with one of hers.

Ah, how many charms that day held for me! It was the most wonderful one in all my life and the first in which I savoured the delights of sensuousness to the full. This memory which causes me so much pleasure brings at the same time the bitterest regrets. But I want to forget about that for the time being.

There reigned in the room an agreeable sultriness, and I was so comfortable the way I was that I did not want to put anything on. I was in such a gay mood that I wanted to have supper naked. Lucette, always on the alert, had had the good sense to dismiss all the servants, and she prepared the meal herself after locking all the doors. Still I was not satisfied. I wanted her to be as we were, and without further ado, I tore off her few garments. She made an enchanting picture. Thus we sat at the table. Seated between the two of us, my father was the object of our fondlings which he gave back in good measure. The mirrors multiplied the charm of the tableau we formed. Our moods and attitudes were varied by our sallies inspired by a delicate wine.

Under its influence our cunts became inflamed and Papa's prick resumed its old stiffness and firmness. In the state of mind we were in, the table no longer pleased us and we hurried back to the bed. During that day, which was consecrated to me, I was plunged once again into the delights of supreme voluptuousness. Papa lay on my left, his legs under my raised ones, and his prick proudly presented itself to the entrance.

Lucette stretched herself out on me, my head between her knees. Her delightful little cunt was just above my eyes; I half-opened it and tickled it while I stroked her buttocks which were stuck up in the air. Her stomach was grazing my breasts and her thighs were between my arms. All was calculated to ignite the flame of passion.

She spread wide the lips of my cunt which was now a deep red. I urged her to put the contraceptive into it so that my father could enjoy me and discharge into me without any worry.

My cunt hurt like anything, and the pain became even worse as soon as it was touched. In spite of this soreness, I endured the procedure with the knowledge that it would be succeeded by sensations more agreeable. Lucette conducted my father's prick onto the path from which she had removed all the dangers and which was now strewn only with flowers. He rushed along it, and quickly sank into the aperture. Her finger was also inside at the same time. I rendered her a similar service while my father was doing the same thing in her cunt with his finger that his prick was doing in mine.

These variations, these positions, and this multiplicity of personages and sensations in the preliminaries enhanced infinitely their delights. Simultaneously we felt them approaching, but ready to escape us like a flash of lightning, and we savoured them to their fullest extent. Now we began to feel fatigue. Lucette, who was the first to get up, set everything in order. As soon as she was back, we returned to the bed and, wrapped in one another's arms, fell back to sleep.

My disappointment that such joys were not to be had every day can be imagined. My father, always solicitous about the state of my health, ordered me back into the chastity belt.

'My dear Laurette,' he explained to me, 'I do not hide from you that I have misgivings about you and all of us. Your character is not yet sufficiently formed so that I can leave you to your own devices, and you are too dear to me for me not to guide your steps for a while longer. Nonetheless, you will have your pleasure from our lovemaking. You'll do it with us, and, in a certain manner, you will share our pleasure. Also, from time to time, we'll reserve for you a similar night, which you will find much more agreeable if you have to wait for it. Finally, if you wish to please me, you will lend yourself to what I desire of you, and you will comply without argument.'

That was his method of rendering my new imprisonment less unbearable.

Nineteen months had passed since that memorable evening when I learned to my sorrow that Lucette was leaving us. Her father, who lived in the provinces and was mortally ill, had summoned her for a last meeting. Her departure caused us the greatest regret. Our sincere tears mingled with hers. As for myself, I could not hold back my sobs, which finally subsided when she said she would return to us as quickly as she could. But shortly after the death of her father, she went into a decline from which it took two years for her to recover. Her father had left her a comfortable inheritance which made her much sought after by the young bachelors of the region, but she would have nothing to do with them. According to her letters, they formed such a contrast with my father that all those who paid her suit, she found absolutely revolting. Marriage was the furthest thing from her mind and her greatest wish was to return to us.

Nevertheless, urged by her mother and other relatives who praised the advantages to be found where she was, and the need that her infirm parent had of her, she was finally persuaded to remain with her family, much against her will, but only after consulting with my father in whom she had the greatest confidence.

Since the suitor who presented himself offered numerous advantages, my father felt himself obliged out of a sense of principle to advise her to accept him, a decision which he found extremely repugnant to make, for he confided in me several times that he had a presentiment of misfortune for her, but to which he could not lend credence, regarding it as a weakness. His foreboding was correct, however, for she died in her first childbirth.

Often I regretted the departure of Lucette, whose loss I regarded as my own, but I consoled myself in the arms of my dear and tender father. I had finally rid myself for good of that detestable attachment I had so often cursed. But what had happened to Lucette because of her excesses weighed heavily on me and made me realize how careful I would have to be because of my delicate constitution. I confided my misgivings to my father, with whom I slept every night. He was never far from me and he watched over me like a guardian angel, stopping me when I yielded to my desires with too much ardour.

After Lucette's departure, he had made some changes in his suite. For example, one could only enter my room by passing through his. Our beds touched against the same wall. Thus not even the servants had the slightest inkling of our frolics.

It was during one of those delightful nights that he enabled me to enjoy a new kind of pleasure, one of which I didn't have the slightest idea. It was marvellous.

'Dearest Laura,' he began. 'You have given me your first flower, but you possess another blossom that you owe me, one you cannot refuse me if you hold me dear.'

'Oh, Papa, you know the depth of my love for you,' I exclaimed. 'What do I have left that you want? Whatever it is, I give it to you with all my heart, and nothing would give me greater pleasure than for you to have it. Your happiness is my only goal.'

'Dear girl,' he replied, deeply moved. 'I am so delighted with you. Your generosity and nobility match your beauty and grace. The soul of voluptuousness resides in you. It presents itself in myriad forms on every part of your body. Your hands, mouth, armpits, breasts and derriere are all cunt.'

'Take your choice. You're the master, and I lend myself to your slightest desire,' I cried.

He made me turn on my left side with my buttocks

facing him. Moistening my asshole and the head of his prick, he inserted it, so very gently. The difficulty of the passage gave us nothing but a new path strewn with accumulated pleasures. Supporting my leg with his raised knee, he masturbated me, sticking his finger in my cunt from time to time. I was almost wild from this exhilaration on both sides. When he sensed that I was on the verge. he quickened his movements, which I seconded with mine. Then I felt the bottom of my backside inundated with a boiling fluid which produced, on my part, an abundant discharge. I relished an ineffable delight. It seemed as if all the parts of my body were fused into one spasm of lust. My convulsions and transports were all due to that incomparable sharp-pointed virility belonging to a man whom I adored.

'What a ravishing pleasure,' sighed my father. 'What do you have to say about it? Judging from your moans and movements, you must have enjoyed it as much as I.'

'Ah, Papa,' I breathed. 'It was infinite, new and strange. How can I put into words all the varied raptures I experienced? What happened before was as nothing to what I just now enjoyed.'

'In that case, my dear child, another time I will employ a dildo to give you new pleasures, ones that you never dreamed of.'

'Papa, what is a dildo?' I innocently asked.

'You'll see,' he mysteriously replied. 'But you'll have to wait until another day.'

The following day, the only thing I talked about was a dildo. I absolutely insisted on seeing one. My persistence was such that he finally acceded to my

57

wishes. I was dumbfounded when he produced it, but I demanded that he try it out on me that very evening. I had to admit it was a poor substitute for the real thing.

There was not one variation of pleasure he did not show me and initiate me into. Sometimes he lay on me, his head between my thighs and mine between his knees. With his open, hot mouth, he covered the lips of my cunt and noisily and greedily sucked them. Then he stuck his tongue deep down between them or with the tip tickled my clitoris. In return, I sucked the head of his prick. Squeezing it with my lips, I soon had it all the way in my mouth. I wished I could have swallowed it. At the same time, I caressed his testicles, his belly, his thighs, and his rump.

'Everything is pleasure and delight, when two people love each other as tenderly and passionately as we do,' he was accustomed to say.

Such was the joyous existence I led after the departure of my beloved governess. Eight or nine months rolled by before I knew it. The only clouds on the horizon were the souvenirs of Lucette. I spent happy days and happier nights in the arms of my adored father whom I overwhelmed with my kisses and embraces. How he cherished me! My soul was united to his, and I loved him in a way no words could express.

If the heart remains constant and is filled with the same sentiments, there is always some phantom caprice which pushes us beyond the limit which we should not exceed and carries us much farther than we ourselves desire to go. I was a striking example of that. Do I dare make that confession? Yes. Nothing must remain hidden. I blush at revealing it to my reader.

We have seen the bounty and goodness of my father towards me, the justness of his spirit, and the steadfastness of his character. In other words, he showed how much he merited my love and heart. His image will never be effaced from my heart.

In our house also lived a kindly, devout, aged widow, who spent the greater part of the day in the neighbouring churches. She had three children, the oldest a debauchee in the fullest sense of the word whose companions were of the lowest order. We scarcely ever saw him. He amused himself by squandering the money he had inherited from his father. His younger brother was about sixteen when he left school to join his mother. He was as adorable as a cherub, with a cheerful temperament and a kindly, gentle character.

As for the sister, she was a honey blonde, with pink-tinted cheeks, sparkling eyes, turned-up nose, vermilion smiling mouth, luscious figure, but petite in build, a madcap if you ever saw one, and possessed of an amorous temperament which she cleverly kept concealed. She constantly joked about the sermons her pious mother gave her from time to time.

I became very close to her after Lucette had left, and I made the acquaintance of her younger brother on the few occasions when he accompanied her. Later, there did not pass a day when they did not come to see me and spend the afternoon or evening with me. Their mother was particularly happy at these visits, for she held me up as a model of virtue to her daughter. It is quite true that I had a reserved air that was both inborn and strengthened by my father's example.

I noticed that my father was studying and making up his mind about Vernol and his sister. One day, he told me that Rose knew more than her nanny had ever taught her, and that if she was less instructed than I in sexual matters, which he doubted, she was eager to learn. Also, he mentioned that if I was curious to find out the extent of her knowledge, I was free to do so. The banter Rose and I exchanged afterwards led me to the same opinion as my father, but I could not figure out Vernol.

My talents had been perfected. I was a good musician, playing the harp with taste and singing with feeling, reciting with feeling and consequently, Rose, Vernol and I formed a little society. During our meetings, he made known the depth of his feelings for me. He sought me out on the slightest pretext and followed me ceaselessly. When he was with me, he was in turn attentive, submissive and impertinent, but all his actions told me what he did not dare say. When I became aware of it, I informed my father. My tone was mocking.

'Laura, the first time I saw him, I guessed. When he is with you, his eyes and cheeks become animated. He does his best to hide his embarrassment, but he is not very successful. You can see right through him. Now that you know his love for you, what feelings do you have for him?'

I had never asked myself that question. Up to then, I had considered Vernol merely my friend, and I always addressed him in such a fashion. But my father's query made me think and, on reflection, I had to admit that I was not unsusceptible to Vernol's presence, and that when he was not with his sister, I sorely missed him. When he was absent, I always eagerly asked Rose where he was and what he was doing. It was a mystery to me how a caprice for the likes of him, who was so unlike me, could have taken hold of me. His handsomeness attracted me, to be sure, and his good manners and his winning ways added to his charms.

From my father's look, it was not hard to see that he had discovered in me what I almost did not dare admit to myself. He went for some time without speaking to me about it. I loved him more than ever for his silence, if that were possible. My admiration and affection did not diminish in the slightest, and as a child of truth and simplicity, I was unable to dissimulate. It is claimed that we women are false by character, but I am of the opinion that this so-called sham is acquired and not inborn. Finally, feeling able to sacrifice everything for my loving father, I made up my mind to avoid the pursuit and attentions of the handsome young lad. I was unable to reconcile in my fantasy the feelings I had for Vernol with those I had for my father.

Apparently, my father wanted to put me to the test (for which I was totally unprepared), because one day he took me aside.

'Laura,' he said to me rather sternly. 'I am not very fond of your new friends. Would you please not see Rose and her brother any more?'

I did not hesitate for an instant. Throwing my arms around his neck and pressing him to my bosom, I sobbed:

'If you say so, dear father. Of course, I won't have anything more to do with them. If you wish, you can send them away, or we can go to the country where I won't be able to see them. Let's leave tomorrow. I'll be ready to go.'

Indeed, I started off to pack my things. I was busy at my task when he called me back. Seating me on his knees, he hugged me tightly and affectionately.

'My dear Laurette,' he stammered with emotion in his voice, 'I am overjoyed at your tenderness and affection for me. Your dry eyes tell me that you are willing to make this sacrifice without any pain. Tell me that it is so, I beg of you. Open your heart to me, for there is no doubt that fear is not at the bottom of your resolution. You have never had to be afraid with me.'

'No, father,' I answered simply, 'I have never been afraid of you. I am just following my feelings. I agree that Vernol has given birth within me to an illusion, a caprice, if you wish, which I cannot explain. But my heart is filled with you. When it comes to you, there is not a moment of indecision. I don't want to see him any more.'

'No, my child,' my father quietly declared. 'I just wanted to learn the nature of your sentiments for me, and now I am satisfied. Vernol excites in you sensations that your imagination enhances. You will enjoy them. Also, you will learn the full extent of my tenderness for you, and you will feel that you cannot stop loving me. And that's all I want. Go ahead. I am only jealous of your heart, the possession of which is so precious to me.'

I was stunned. I fell at his knees, my face bathed

in tears and my bosom heaving. I was sobbing so violently that I could barely speak.

'Dearest Papa,' I stuttered, 'I love you and I adore you. In my heart, there is only room for you.'

He was deeply moved at my grief. Raising me up and pressing me to him in turn, he covered my face with kisses.

'Console yourself, my child. Don't you think that I know nature and its immutable laws? Follow your heart, for, as you know, I am not hard-hearted. It is time for you to learn the difference between fatherly love and the love of a lover. I promised you that you will enjoy pleasure with Vernol. As you well know, I keep my word. Besides, he is a nice lad, good-looking and well-mannered. That I have to say for him. If your heart had not gone out to him, it would have turned to someone else, perhaps not as worthy as he. That is the reason for my decision.'

From that day, I felt myself much freer with Vernol. After spending one night in my father's arms, I awoke to hear him telling me between the kisses I was raining on his cheeks that I should pay a call on Rose's mother.

'Tell her to allow her daughter to spend the day in the country with you, and mention, too, that she should not worry if she does not return in the evening for we'll bring her back the next day. As an excuse, we'll say that the coach is being repaired, and you'll keep her here until tomorrow. When you are alone with her, you can find out her inclinations and what she does. She seems to trust you. Once you have wormed your way into her confidence, let me know.'

For a moment, I thought he had designs on her,

but I did not ask any questions. I merely did what I was bidden. For some time, I suspected that Rose was as knowledgeable as I, or almost.

Everything went as my father planned. She came and the door was locked to all comers. All alone, we spent the day in the maddest follies. I played a hundred mischievous tricks on her. She returned them with interest. I bared her budding bosom and made my father kiss the pink-nosed puppies. Her buttocks, her *mons Veneris* and her cunt suffered my playful tortures. I held her in my arms so that my father could repeat my performance, at which she laughed and giggled. Although at times she pretended indignation at some unexpected prank, she lent herself willingly to everything we could think of. Her eyes were glistening and her cheeks flushed.

I partook only sparingly of the collation that was served, but I kept filling her glass to stoke the flames that were already consuming her. After rising from the table, we renewed our frolics. Rose, no longer capable of any resistance, was turned over with her face down on a settee. I raised her skirts, and her bared behind presented a perspective that no painter's brush could reproduce. My father helped me to get revenge for all the tricks she had played on me. I was curious to learn what effect these games would have on her, and when I looked more closely, I found she was almost dripping between her thighs. No doubt about it. She had enjoyed herself immensely during our madcap pranks.

Finally, Rose and I went to my room where we got ready to go to bed. As soon as she saw me in my chemise, she tore it off me. I did the same to her, hurling the last garment to the floor. Dragging me to the bed, she gave me long drawn-out kisses as she fondled my straining breasts and damp matted mount. Immediately, I put my finger on the spot which I guessed would give her the most pleasure. I was not mistaken. She spread her legs and kept cadence with the movement of my finger. Still curious, I inserted my finger into her cunt, and the ease with which it entered left no doubt as to the use she had made of it.

Now I was burning to find out how and when she had lost her maidenhead. I was just about to question her when my father entered the room to kiss us good-night before retiring. With a sudden jerk, Rose threw off the covers, revealing us completely in the nude with our hands on each other's centres of voluptuousness. She put her arms around his neck, drew his head down, and made him kiss my breasts. Not to be outdone, I forced him to do the same to her seductive gloves. Then I promenaded his hand all over her body, stopping it only at her Venus mount. I could see that he was aroused, but he left us abruptly, wishing us an amusing night.

The clock was striking ten when, the next morning, my father returned to our room and asked, as he awakened us, if we had had a pleasant night.

'We stayed up long after you left, Papa. You saw the mood we were in when you left us.'

Rose, whom our diversions had calmed and sleep had refreshed, blushed and clapped her hand to my mouth. I promptly removed it.

'No, Rose,' I declared, 'you will never prevent me from telling my father everything we did and all you told me. I never conceal anything from him, for I trust him implicitly, as he does me.'

Placing her arms and legs around me, she allowed me to continue.

'When you left us, Papa, Rose was already at a high pitch of excitement. As soon as we were alone, she kissed me passionately on the mouth and began to suck hard on my nipples. She drew me close to her, on top of her. Our legs were interlocked so that our cunts were rubbing one another. My breasts were dangling and grazing hers, and we were belly to belly. Demanding my tongue, she cuddled my buttocks with one hand and with the other tickled my clitoris. By the action of her finger, she invited me to do the same to her. I put my finger on the spot where she was waiting impatiently, and soon we experienced the delights of these amusements. But she refused to let me withdraw it until she had enjoyed ineffable transports four times.'

While I was rendering an account of our gambols, Rose, aroused again by the description and the recollection, had inserted her hand between my thighs and performed what I was telling. I immediately grasped what she was desiring. We had remained in the nude, and I uncovered her. Then I grasped my father's hand which immediately took possession of all her charms. All he was wearing was a dressing-gown which half opened at his movements. From the protuberance straining against the cloth, I could see the effect that the touch of his hands on her body was producing on him. Pointing it out to Rose, I advised her to take off his robe and lay him at our sides. Unhesitatingly, she got up, threw herself at him, stripped him and, enveloping him in her arms, pushed him on the bed.

I was not idle, for I lifted one of her legs on him, and passed the other through his. In this position, his prick naturally was face to face with her cunt, and it goes without saying that I guided the member on its proper route. Her anticipation was so great that she began to quiver like a willow in the wind. With an upward thrust of her derriere, she precipitated the entry into the venereal temple. I fondled her most sensitive parts, an activity she seconded with perfect rhythm. From her passionate transports, we could perceive the excessive pleasure she was undergoing.

My father, who was experiencing the keenness with which she was sucking his prick, was unable to hold himself back. He hurriedly withdrew, and with my hand I finished off the libation that he feared to empty into Rose's cunt. In a delirium, Rose moaned that she had discharged five times while he was in her. Her stomach was inundated with the fuck he was spreading on her. It went all the way up to her breasts. While I was attending to these various duties, she took hold of my cunt which she began to titillate. This little game, together with the emotions caused by the sight of their bliss and the fondlings I was lavishing on them, soon put me in a state of violent agitation.

Now I fervently desired the fire that was devouring me to be quenched. Rose was quick to notice it, and she soon enabled me to join in the merriment.

When we had somewhat recovered from our exertions, I found enough breath to address my father.

'Listen, Papa,' I murmured. You are probably as astounded as I was at Rose's skill, and I won her promise to tell me where and how she had received her training. Now I am going to repeat to you her story, but, no, it is from her mouth that you are going to hear it, and I hope that she is agreeable. What you have just done with her puts her in just the mood to tell you everything without embarrassment and to confide in you all of what she said to me.'

Embraces and kisses were sufficient to overcome her feeble protests.

'Well, all right. Since Laura knows everything already, I have nothing to lose. From what I have gathered, even if I did not impart my story to you, you would get it from Laurette. Moreover, I trust you completely after what we have been through. Yes, it is better that I tell you myself.'

# PART III

'I was sixteen years old when my mother sent me to one of her sisters in the provinces, where I spent six months, mostly in the company of her daughter who was a year my senior. Until that time, I had led a secluded life, always with my mother who is so pious that she never mixes with other people. Since my brothers were away at school, I was either alone or at church with my mother. As you can imagine, I was bored to tears.

'Nevertheless, I liked it better in church than at home, because, although my mother and I sat in the most remote corner in the house of worship, I was aware that someone now and then would have his eyes fixed on me.

'Quite some time before, my mother had promised her sister to send me to her for a stay, since she had often said she would like to have me. I was very eager to go, because I knew that my aunt was the exact opposite of my stuffy mother. It was, however, an unforeseen turn of events that finally caused my

71

mother to keep her word. My oldest brother, who was at home at the time, had contracted the pox, and it was imperative that I leave the house as quickly as possible.

'My aunt and cousin welcomed me with the utmost cordiality. Immediately after a warm exchange of hugs and kisses, Isabelle, for that was my cousin's name, insisted that I share her bed. Although I may have constrained her at the beginning, she embraced me tenderly every night before we went to sleep, and in the morning, when we awoke, I returned her tokens of affection.

'It was not two weeks until we were such warm friends that in the evening in bed, she tucked up our nightgowns to press her buttocks against mine and then give me the four sisters' kiss.

'One night, when I could not fall asleep, although I pretended to, I felt Isabelle's arm make a slight movement. Now her hand was on the upper part of my thigh. Her breathing was heavy and spasmodic, while her derriere gave little twitches. Finally, after a deep sigh, she calmed down and went to sleep.

'Bewildered by her strange behaviour, I at first thought that there might be something wrong with her. The next morning, however, she was her cheerful self, and my anxiety vanished. From that time on, I was aware that she was acting the same way every night. It was a mystery to me, but it was not long before I was to be enlightened.

'My aunt had a chambermaid of about twenty with whom Isabelle was often alone in her room, ostensibly because Justine embroidered beautifully and Isabelle was taking lessons from her. My cousin told me never to disturb her when she was with Justine, for the work required the greatest concentration. At first, I swallowed the story, but when I noticed that she had become as skilful as her teacher, I became suspicious.

'To tell the truth, I was also piqued at being excluded from these tête-à-têtes, and I determined to get to the bottom of the matter. For a young girl, curiosity is the tormenting demon to whom she has to yield lest she succumb herself.

'One day, I found myself all alone in the house, my aunt having gone out with Isabelle, and Justine away doing some errands. Taking advantage of their absence, I went into Isabelle's room to see if I could not find some way whereby I could learn what was going on in there when they were by themselves. After exploring the room, I spied near the foot of my cousin's bed an almost hidden door that I was able to open only after several vigorous jerks. It led into a dim chamber filled with old furniture heaped up almost to the ceiling. The only free space was a narrow passage going to another portal which opened onto a concealed staircase that descended down to a little courtyard from which one emerged into a deserted alley.

'If my aunt thought that she had shut off this part of the house, Isabelle or Justine undoubtedly had discovered the keys. In the furniture-jammed room, I noticed in the wall a bit of drapery that seemed to cover some aperture into my cousin's room. Climbing up on a dusty chair to investigate further, I found a little hole in the cloth through which I could look into the adjoining room. Since it was too small to afford a clear view, I took my scissors and enlarged it so that nothing obstructed my vision. Delighted with my stratagem and determined to take full advantage of it, I beat a quick retreat, closing the door behind me. As I returned to my room, I recalled that when Justine went to Isabelle's room, it was almost always after lunch.

'The opportunity I was waiting for finally came when my aunt went to pay a call on an old friend. Since the matter she wished to discuss was of a delicate nature, she did not take Isabelle or myself. When she was gone, Isabelle made a point of telling me that because she had some new intricate stitch to learn with Justice, I was to feel free to do as I wished as long as she was not disturbed. That was all I needed.

'I made as if I were going for a stroll, but in reality I stealthily made my way to the unlit room, where I hid myself among the discarded pieces of furniture and fastened my eye to the opening. Not long after, I saw my cousin come in with some embroidery in her hand. At the sight of that my heart sank, for I was sure that I was going to spend a boring afternoon and I repented of my curiosity.

'But my hopes rose when Justine appeared and immediately asked where I was. Isabelle replied I had gone to see some friends in the vicinity. Reassured, the maid quickly latched the bedroom door and opened the one of the room in which I was concealed, continuing to the hidden staircase.

'I shook with fright at the thought of being discovered, but she apparently did not notice me as she groped her way down the passage. On her return, Isabelle put aside her work and went to the mirror to arrange her hair. When she began to readjust her scarf and blouse, Justine snatched them off, revealing my cousin's snowy bosom. Taking one of the pink-tipped globes in her hands, she complimented my cousin on their roundness and firmness. Then, baring her own full hemispheres, she compared them to Isabelle's.

'As they were thus amusing themselves, I heard somebody coming up the staircase. Because of the way I was crouched down, I could not see him as he passed by my hiding place. On hearing a scratch at the door, Justine opened the door and then quickly closed it again.

'As soon as the stranger was in the room, I immediately recognized him. He was a tall young fellow slightly related to the family and he paid us an occasional call. His name was Courbelon. Isabelle was not at all embarrassed when he went up and kissed her still uncovered bosom. At the same time, his hand went up under her skirt. When he had finished, he gave Justine the same greeting.

'Taking Isabella up in his arms, he lay her at the foot of the bed where he threw up her skirt to reveal her all. From my vantage point, I could see her flat stomach, her slightly plump thighs, and her rose-lipped slit. She did not have much hair down there, but what there was of it was pitch black. Putting his mouth to the orifice, he tickled its upper part with his finger which soon disappeared in its depths.

'In the meantime, Justine unbuttoned the front of his trousers and brought out an organ of astonishing dimensions which my cousin shamelessly grasped. As he began to replace the finger with it, I heard Justine scold him: "No Courbelon, that I won't allow. If I were to get pregnant, I would know what to do to avoid unpleasant consequences, but if Isabelle ever got into that condition, where could the two of us hide ourselves? Caress and fondle her as much as you like, but just don't you dare put that into her."

'That discourse, which I heard distinctly, was a complete enigma for me. I saw Courbelon reluctantly withdraw the member and grumblingly titillate Isabelle, who was clutching his masculinity as she had before.

'A short time after he had resumed the game with his fingers, I heard and saw the same sighs and motions that she made when we two were in bed together.

'Now I had a glimmering of what had been happening. She had been doing to herself what Courbelon was now doing to her. Now that it was over, Isabelle rose from the bed, and Justine, who had been watching them like a hawk, threw herself in turn on the couch. With one arm she embraced the small of Courbelon's back, and with the other she gripped the truncheon as she dragged him down on her. In a twinkling of the eye, her skirt was up to her navel. Resting on her stomach, he massaged the pearl-shaped breasts which he then covered with feverish kisses. Judging from the convulsive movements of her flanks and derriere, I gathered he was inserting his member into her. I would have given anything to see it go in.

'From behind, my cousin passed her hand between his bucking buttocks, either to fondle his testicles or to measure how deep the member had penetrated.

Now both were seized by spasms. They must have been in seventh heaven. It seemed that Courbelon was dying after a violent explosion. When he pulled out his instrument, it was no longer its proud self, but a humble, self-effacing creature diminished in length and thickness. I thought it rather resembled an earthworm. Exhausted, they paused for several moments on the bed, after which the kisses and embraces were resumed.

'This opening scene, which thoroughly delighted me, was soon followed by a second act which aroused my emotions even more.

'Impatient with their hampering garments and aware that my aunt would not be back until dusk, Courbelon tore off their clothing, and in an instant they both were as naked as the day they were born. In proportion, Justine's figure was not the equal of Isabelle's, but her skin was whiter and more satiny and her body more rounded and contoured. Playing no favourites, his lips alternated rapidly between the bodies of his two enticing partners. And their bottoms, breasts and slits were his to do with as he wished.

'What I regarded avidly for more than half an hour lit fires within me and excited emotions I had never before experienced. The caresses of the intertwined trio became more animated. Now Courbelon made his two lovely partners lie on their backs, side by side, then on their bellies, with their legs spread wide apart. I saw as clearly as Courbelon all that met his eyes. He examined them carefully, kissed their slightly arched buttocks, and stuck a finger of each hand between their thighs. In the meantime, his instrument was restored to its pristine condition.

'Because Justine could not see him from the position she was in, Courbelon took advantage of the situation to introduce the monstrosity into Isabelle. Suddenly, however, Justine became mistrustful and abruptly sat up. When she saw what he was doing, she grabbed the miscreant by the neck, nearly choking him, and dragged him off of his willing victim.

'I was furious, for I was following the course of the implement with the deepest interest, and Justine had to ruin it all.

' "No, no," she stated firmly. That is not permitted. I've told you the reason a hundred times, and you're just going to have to give up the idea."

'Since I could hear as clearly as I could see, I did not miss a single word or phrase.

' "Come now, my dear boy!" Justine said in a conciliatory tone as she took hold of the offender. "Why don't you just put your prick into my cunt? They are old friends, and you don't run any risk with me!"

'She was too late, though. Before inserting it in her, she gave it two or three shakes. At that, I saw Courbelon lean on her shoulder, holding one of her breasts and kissing it, as he spilled out a white liquid I had never seen before. The spurts were accompanied by a series of convulsions that marked the depth of his rapture. For some unknown reason, the sight nearly drove me out of my mind.

'Without realizing it, I had been irritating the upper part of my slit in the same fashion I had seen Courbelon do to Justine and Isabelle. I was engaged in this stimulating occupation which gave me nothing but unalloyed pleasure. Suddenly, Justine and my cousin, undoubtedly animated by the caresses he had lavished on them, put him in the same state they themselves were in, namely, complete stark nudity. From head to toe, there was not a stitch of clothing on his body.

'This new perspective attracted my eyes to him with a delicious curiosity, for unknowingly, that is just the way I had wanted to see him. As I regarded them, it seemed that their enjoyments were all that I had ever desired. Justine and Isabelle were caressing him, kissing him, fondling the now lifeless virility, and cuddling his testicles and buttocks. In return, he kissed them, massaged and sucked their nipples, turned them over on their backs, looked minutely at their rear cheeks, and excited them by inserting and withdrawing his fingers in and out of their apertures.

'As this went on, I noticed his instrument slowly regaining all its former pride. The organ, with which he playfully menaced the laughing girls, looked like a pike about to be stuck into the body of a ferocious beast. There was no mistaking Courbelon's desire for my cousin, but Justine, taking a firm hold on him, forced him with her back down on top of the bed. For a moment, I thought he was going to split open her stomach, but she was not to be daunted.

' "Let's wait a moment," he suggested to her, "so that we may enjoy our raptures simultaneously."

'Placing Isabelle on the bed, he spread open her knees and thighs between which Justine put her legs, also spread apart. Since there was nothing to hinder my view, I was able to see Courbelon's truncheon sink into her aperture, only to reappear, vanish again, and so on.

'It seemed inconceivable that such a fearsome object could ever enter my opening, which was so tight I could barely get my little finger into it. And I never dared push it too far because of the sheer agony it caused. But Justine's example lent me courage, and I determined not to worry about the consequences, no matter what they would be.

'While Courbelon had his prick in Justine's cunt, his finger was ensconced in Isabelle's. He turned my cousin's head by telling her that she possessed the most charming Venus mount he had ever beheld. After saying the same about her slit, he recommended her to stimulate her clitoris, a suggestion she promptly followed as he slipped his finger in and out in regular cadence with his thrusts into Justine.

'Steadfast in my determination to follow their example, at least in part, I took a deep breath and plunged in the forefinger of my left hand as deep as I could, all the while stirring it around in imitation of the movement of Courbelon's prick. Gradually, a delicious sensation invaded my whole being, and I now realized why my cousin took such a pleasure in a repetition of the game.

'It was not long before the trio was wallowing in utter ecstasy. Isabelle, still on her back, was wiggling her backside like a shimmy-dancer from the South Seas. Witnessing her transports, Courbelon suddenly shouted in glee: "Darling, you're coming!"

'Scarcely had he finished uttering these words than he fell almost senseless on Justine's bountiful bosom after sighing deeply and mouthing oaths to describe his bliss. Justine, after agitatedly twitching her rump, also remained prostrate.

'These evidences of impassioned enjoyments roused me to such a pitch of excitement that I, too, sank back exhausted against a piece of furniture, undergoing at the same time an ineffable gratification. What an excess of delight to feel for the first time such a hitherto unknown voluptuousness, a delight never dreamed of. Such bliss lifts one out of this world and, for too brief a period, it is the only thing that really exists.

'During the subsequent period when I was savouring to the full my complete contentment, the three performers in the adjoining room were starting to put back on their clothes. As soon as they were decent, Courbelon tenderly embraced the two girls and made his way out as he had come in. A few moments later, Justine and Isabelle also left the room. As for myself, I waited a while longer to emerge from my place of concealment and, taking the same route as Courbelon, I regained the inhabited part of the house. Shortly afterwards, my aunt returned in company with Isabelle, who had gone out to meet her.

'From that time on, I thought and dreamed of nothing but what I had witnessed. Their words were still ringing in my ears and their actions were still before my eyes. Not for a moment were my reflections far from that living tableau.

'That very evening when I was in bed with Isabelle, I pretended that I was sound asleep and Isabelle fell in a profound slumber. Since it was apparent that she was not going to do anything to me, I had to seek resources within myself, and I followed her example. But the following evening was an entirely different affair.

'As soon as we were in bed and my cousin thought I was asleep, I became aware that she was starting her little game again. Knowing now full well what was going on, I turned over and, placing my thigh on hers, I put my hand where I knew she had her finger. I slid it under and immediately had her whole mound in my palm. As I fondled her tenderly, I kissed her budding breasts and inserted my finger into her slit. Then I withdrew it to tickle the spot where I had found hers. When she spread her legs and let me have my way with her, I heard her abruptly heave a deep sigh and, to my amazement, I found her all wet in the area where my hand was.

'Now overcome with the urge for the same to be done to me, I gripped her hand and covered my own hillock with it. Forcing her digital extremity to do its duty, I soon found myself returning sigh for sigh.

'She was not a little surprised at all I was doing, for she believed me as innocent as the day I was born. Knowing that I had been raised in a strait-laced puritanical home, she had been wary about imparting to me any of her secrets for fear I would blab everything to my aunt or mother.

' "Well, Rose, how is it that you are so experienced?" she asked curiously. "I am really amazed."

' "That I can believe, my dear cousin, and I'll tell you on the condition that you won't be angry with me and that you will keep on loving me," I replied.

'The moment I said it, I regretted having opened my mouth and was reluctant to continue until Isabelle, taking me in her arms, tenderly pressed me to go on and tell her all.

' "You aren't afraid of me, are you?' she asked. "I

assure you that you can count on my discretion, and I solemnly promise never to say a word, particularly not to our mothers."

'Reassured, I recounted all I had witnessed and how I was able to be a witness. When I had finished, she was aghast at what I had learned.

' "Oh, Rose, my dear Rose, I beg you never to reveal my secret. If you betray me, I'm lost."

'I vowed to be as silent as the grave, and my cousin said she was not even going to tell Justine that I knew. After I had calmed her fears, she rained kisses on my face and body, all the while questioning me closely on what I had seen and heard and the impression it had made on me. I gave her a full account, including my own reaction. Now that she knew of my own misdeeds, her last lingering doubts vanished. Now it was my turn to satisfy my own curiosity.

' "But tell me, Isabelle, how did you happen to fall in with Justine and Courbelon?"

' "I'll do so gladly, cousin," she replied. "Since you know everything, there is little point in holding anything back, and besides, I am sure that you will not break your promise.

' "About four or five weeks before you came here, I had gone out with my mother to pay some calls, but having forgotten my bag in my room, I went back alone to get it. After I found it, I went to Justine's room for some reason or another. Since the door was partially open, I entered without knocking.

' "What met my eyes nearly stunned me. I was stupefied to find Courbelon on top of her in the strangest position. When he noticed me, he quickly got off his mount, but not before I saw his organ

83

which he hurriedly tried to conceal at the same time he was lowering Justine's skirts that were up to her navel. Although she was dismayed at being discovered, she was relieved that it was not my mother who had found out her guilty secret. I began to leave right away, but Justine, fearing that I would tell what I had seen, ran after me, got on her knees, and begged me with tears in her eyes not to reveal her shameful disgrace. Her pleas were so heart-rending that I promised all that she wanted and kept my word.

' "I'll admit to you, dear Rose, that the incident gave rise to many thoughts and conjectures which kept running through my head. From that time on, Justine often came to my room under the pretext of giving me embroidery lessons, but, in reality, the instruction was of a completely different sort. She taught me things I had never dreamed of. She bared my bosom and played with my breasts as she depicted in the most vivid colours the delights of sensual pleasure. I have to admit that I was all ears.

' "Finally, one day, her descriptions so aroused my curiosity and latent sensuousness that my cheeks were flaming, my breath was coming in short gasps, and my bosom was rising and falling. The eager questions I threw at her enabled her to sense that the moment she had been waiting for had come. She took me in her arms, lifted me up, and bore me to the bed, where she raised my skirts. Vaguely sensing that she wished to play forbidden games, I feebly tried to stop her, but she was undeterred, telling me that any handsome young cavalier would be overjoyed to be in her place and regard and touch the beauties she was gradually exposing. His organ would swell and then he would expire rapturously, giving me at the same time the most unimaginable delights. Her flattery, lascivious descriptions and caresses had completely reduced my defences, and I let her do with me as her fancy dictated.

' "Then she placed the tip of the finger of her left hand between the lips of my opening which she titillated, while with the right she rubbed my clitoris."

' "My dear cousin," I interrupted her, "why don't you call a spade a spade and use the terms I heard Justine and Courbelon employ?"

' "You're right, Rose," she conceded. "I should have remembered that I don't have to be careful about my language with you.

' "After some moments of this treatment, I finally experienced that supreme sensation she had described in such glowing terms, even though she told me that the pleasure would be tenfold greater with a gallant young man. Ever since then, we have often been playing this delightful game, much to my satisfaction. One day, she went so far as to stick her finger in me. I felt some pain at first, but it soon went away. It was not long before she was teaching me how to return the favours she was bestowing on me, which I did, and not simply out of a sense of gratitude.

' "A week or so before your arrival, my mother went to make some calls without me, enabling Justine and me to resume our joyful diversions, but this time we were completely in the nude. I did not know it, but Courbelon was hidden behind a curtain witnessing all our merry pranks. As I was to learn later, it had been planned between him and Justine.

' "As he emerged from his place of concealment,

also in the nude, Justine nearly burst her sides laughing to see him in such a state, but I nearly fainted when my eyes caught his enormous erect sceptre. I wanted to flee, but my feet refused to move. Besides, bare as I was, I could hardly leave the room. Trembling and filled with shame and fright, I tried to take refuge behind the curtain, but as I made for it, the two of them stopped me in my tracks. After what Courbelon had seen Justine and I doing, I could scarcely put up an effective resistance.

' "Courbelon held me tightly in his arms, passionately kissed me, and ran his hands and lips all over my quivery body. Finally, my shame gave place to desire. He put the baton in my hand, but it was so thick that my fingers could not encompass it. The fire of his kisses and caresses and the sight of Justine fondling his muscular body set me ablaze, and I was in no state to refuse him anything he wanted. The joys into which he plunged me were so profound that I almost lost consciousness. Justine acted as his able assistant.

' "But the two of them did not stop there. Dragging me to the bed and holding me down with one hand, she made me look at Courbelon's prick which was losing itself in her cunt. From the vivacious expressions on their faces, I had a fair guess of the bliss they were undergoing.

' "Yesterday was the sixth time they allowed me to have the pleasure of their company. You can imagine that we would have had more gatherings had it not been for the fear of discovery. When I learned of your forthcoming visit I was overjoyed, for I hoped your being here would give me more freedom. I confess I was mad to have Courbelon do to me what he always did to Justine, even though Justine had repeatedly warned me of the dangers of pregnancy and I was still awed by the proportions of the desired object.

' "But on closer reflection, I noticed that it caused her no pain. The suffering must be less than the pleasure. Consequently, I decided that my fears were groundless, particularly when Courbelon reassured me on that point. Justine was adamant, but it was hard for me to believe what she said when she was always doing exactly that which she prohibited me."

'When she paused for breath, I urged Isabelle to gratify me as she had been. At first she refused, but I used every argument my innocent mind could come up with. I know that they were not very convincing, but I did not let up. Whether from curiosity, fantasy or coincidence of desire, I do not know, but she finally yielded. From that time, we enjoyed almost nightly what we called our "secret", and we became inseparable.

'A little later, we were invited to a wedding in the village, the bride being a relative of Justine who would be sure to attend. Isabelle laughingly mentioned that it would be a good opportunity to put one over on her Cerberus, for I had been continually urging her to find a way to realize her ambitions with Courbelon. Now was her chance, I told her, and she should not let it go by. I added that my aunt, believing we would be at the celebration together, would take advantage of our absence to visit with friends. All Isabelle had to do was stay in her room, while I went to the wedding, where I surely would find Courbelon. As soon as I saw him, I would tell him that Isabelle was waiting for him to discuss an important matter and that he should go to her room.

'At first, she shook her head and said blushingly that she could not do such a thing. But I kept after her, and with my caresses which stimulated her desires, I prevailed in the end.

'My aunt had already left when I walked to the village. The first person I saw among the merry throng in the banquet room was Courbelon, to whom I gave unnoticed the message from Isabelle. As soon as I had finished, he was gone in a flash. Momentarily, I regretted not being at my observation post, but I consoled myself with the thought that Isabelle would render me a detailed account of all that took place and abandoned myself to the pleasures of the ball.

'When Justine spotted me alone, she immediately inquired why Isabelle was not with me. I replied that I thought she was with her mother for a while, but that she would surely return soon to take part in the festivities. Justine swallowed the story hook, line and sinker, but as time went by and there was no sign of Courbelon, she became suspicious. It was obvious that Courbelon's absence and Isabelle's tardiness were causing her to smell a rat.

'When she seemed at the end of her patience, Courbelon made his appearance, followed by Isabelle a few minutes later. At the sight of them, Justine immediately vanished. I guessed that she had surmised Isabelle had just come from the house. When she came back, there was nothing to be read on her face, but, as we later learned, she had made some inquiries, the answers to which gave her all the information she needed.

'Isabelle turned down all invitations to dance, and when she whispered in my ear the reason, I loudly declared that I, too, was tired from the exertions and was ready to go home. After asking our farewells, we walked back together to my aunt's house. You can imagine my impatience at hearing what had happened, and it seemed an eternity until we were in bed.

'When I tried to put my hand on the spot which should have undergone the assault, she pushed it rudely away, saying that it hurt too much to be touched. There was a moment of silence before the whole story poured forth like water rushing over a dam.

' "Ah, my dear Rose, my curiosity has been satisfied,' she said in a woeful tone. 'Courbelon came promptly to my room when I was eagerly awaiting him. As soon as he opened the door, I flung my arms around his neck and wet his face with my kisses. In turn, he fondled and explored every corner and recess of my body, without my putting up the slightest semblance of resistance. After these preliminaries, he inserted his hard baton in my hole that he had lubricated with his saliva, but you have no idea of what torture it was. That monstrous member was tearing me apart. Not daring to scream, I burst into tears.

' "He tried his best to comfort me by assuring me that the next time I would experience nothing but pure unadulterated bliss, but he deceived me again the second time. His following attack resulted in nothing but redoubled anguish for me. I suffered the unbearable. When he presented himself the third time, I refused him outright, but he was so insistent with his kisses and embraces that I had to yield to his entreaties. He was as gentle and tender as he could be, but it did not help. I could not stand the torment any longer. The stabbing pains along with the fear of getting big with child so terrified me that I shoved him from me with such violence that he did not dare try again. Right now, it feels as if there is fire burning between my thighs. That is why, as I told you, I just could not dance."

' "My darling cousin," I told her consolingly, "since you are younger that Justine, it is quite natural that yours is much tighter and narrower than hers."

' "That's what Courbelon told me. He said that with time and practice my slit would get wider, but in the meantime I am suffering the agonies of hell."

'When she had finished, it was late, and we were so tired that we fell into a deep sleep almost immediately.

'The next day Justine called Isabelle into her room where she simply told her that Courbelon had been in my cousin's room the night before and that the door to the hidden staircase was not locked as it should have been. Moreover, on the rug she had found some petals of the boutonniere he had been wearing. If that were not enough, she found the bed rumpled as if two people had romped on it. Finally, she had learned that Isabelle had not been with her mother, as I had said, but had remained in her room before she left the house more than two hours after I had.

'Although she realized Justine knew what had gone on, she refused to admit it. But the evidence was so damning and Justine was so persistent that she finally made a clean breast of it.

'Either fearing what the consequences might be to

Isabelle or angry at Courbelon for his behaviour, Justine put so many obstacles in their way that they scarcely had a chance to speak to each other, let alone to be by themselves. There was no doubt that Justine was also jealous. Whatever the case may have been, she employed every means at her disposal to break up the affair and watched over their every movement.

'Because of these blockades placed on the road of true love by Justine, Courbelon finally became irritated with his mistress, with whom he soon had a falling out. When he had to move to a remote province, he quickly forgot her as well as Isabelle. Shortly thereafter, Justine left both my aunt's service and the village. Isabelle suspected that she had given up her post to rejoin Courbelon, for whose sake she would have made any sacrifice.

'At first, Isabelle was almost inconsolable at losing him. Whenever we were alone, she always turned the conversation to him. Although I was getting sick and tired of hearing the same old thing day in and day out, I comforted her the best I could and in the end, I succeeded. The pleasures we shared enabled her to bear her loss with more fortitude, and finally she had dismissed him completely from her mind. I have to admit that I was sorry at losing him, for I had entertained high hopes of participating sooner or later in their gambols. But her ever-growing affection for me soon effaced his memory.

'All together, we spent four delightful months in each other's company. During this time, she instructed me in everything she had learned from her former teachers and soon we were able to add a few embellishments of our own.

'Thinking back on this period of my life and the answers Isabelle gave me to the many questions I plied her with made me realize that Courbelon probably had had designs on Isablle from the very day she discovered him with Justine. It seems likely he had persuaded Justine that the best way to guarantee Isabelle's silence was to admit her into their games, and she fell into the trap. If it had not been for her jealousy and mistrust, he most likely would have gained his ends.

'The time that I spent at my aunt's sped by all too quickly. I knew it had to come sooner or later, but I almost burst into tears when my mother wrote saying that she wanted me back with her. My departure was a lachrymose one on all sides. My aunt was so touched that she promised to do everything she could to have me return. Since Isabelle and my aunt knew how to enjoy life, their hearts went out to me, because they envisaged my spending bleak, dreary days with my devout mother who had no social life whatsoever. That was what I thought, also, but the way things turned out proved us all wrong.

'Once back with my mother, I turned to account everything chance and Isabelle had taught me. Like her, I was able to procure for myself the most delicious pleasures every day. More often than not, I allowed myself a double measure. My stimulated imagination was concentrated on one thing, and on one thing only: a man. Every time I came near one, I could not keep my eyes from him. It mattered not if he were young or old – I wanted him to quench the flames that were consuming my entire being.

'Just about that time, my brother Vernol came

home for his vacation. The first thing I noticed was how handsome he had become. That surprised me for apparently his charms had escaped me before. It is true that we always had a good brother and sister relationship, but now I found that my feelings for him had changed completely. In him were united all my yearnings, embers that unknowingly he was stoking. I had eyes only for him.

'For a long time I itched to have him touch and fondle that which I had only let Courbelon glimpse, but I was humble enough to believe that I was too young to be able to attract the attentions of an older man. Besides. I was positive that his male organ had grown in size during his absence, and the thought of Isabelle's trial momentarily frightened me. But that cloud on the horizon quickly passed: and I determined that I was going to have Vernol.

'His room was behind my mother's where I also slept, and when that devout woman departed for church where she spent two or three hours every morning, I quickly locked the door after her. The servants, believing that we were still sleeping, never bothered us. That was my opportunity to go to his room while I was still in my nightgown and tease and annoy him in a thousand ways while he was still in bed. I kissed and tickled him. Other times I would yank off the blankets and sheets so that he was almost naked and then playfully spank his backside which was as soft and tender as a girl's.

'When he had enough, he would leap out of bed and start chasing me. Usually, I let him catch me, whereupon he threw me back on his bed where he paid me back in full for the slaps I had given him.

'We had given ourselves up to these games for two mornings when, on the third, the sport took a different turn. That time, when he hurled me on the bed, my nightgown flew up to my waist (with a little help from me). He looked at me and then at my little cunt. He seemed stunned. Recovering himself after a few moments, he first feasted his eyes on my thighs, gingerly touching them with his hands, and then spread them apart. I made no protest.

' "Ah, Rose," he exclaimed. "This is the first time I have noticed what a difference there is between us."

' "What do you mean, difference?" I innocently replied, feigning ignorance.

' "Take a look for yourself," he cried excitedly as if he had just made a great discovery. With that, he pulled down his trousers and showed me his little implement that I had only half seen before. Under my gaze, it grew in length and rigidity.

'Taking the lance in my hand, I stared at it carefully, tenderly stroked it, pulled the foreskin back and gently rubbed the tip.

' "Let me look at you some more," Vernol begged, impatient to do the same to me.

'More than willing to grant his request, I lay back again on the bed. Raising and spreading my legs, he scrutinized my private parts with the attention of a scientist peering into a microscope, but it was obvious that he had not the faintest idea of their functions. Now he was on his knees, bent over me. Running my hand between his thighs, I grasped the pretty pigmy and amused myself by taking off and putting back on the hat covering the coral head.

'The pleasure I perceived I was giving him

augmented mine, and I was all agog. Straightening up, I reversed him on his back as I completely bared the toy to my view. I kissed it, I nibbled it, and I caressed its little olives. Finally, by means of rubbing my hand up and down on the erect baton, I succeeded in releasing that white fluid I had seen Justine's hand produce with Courbelon. I could not get over the delightful sight of the jets making an arc in the air. He looked as if he did not believe what was happening. In his regard astonishment was mingled with bliss. His hand on my thighs became crisp and then remained motionless.

'Reclining on the pillows, I put my arms around him and made him do a little thing he was totally ignorant of but which I was dying to have. He obliged, and I was soon in that state of ecstasy in which I had put him.

'I was delighted at how extraordinary he found all that was happening, for I had led him from surprise to surprise. I resumed my sweet attack on his innocence by fondling again his instrument, which I then began to kiss and suck. I had it all the way in my mouth. If I could have swallowed it, I would have cheerfully done so. Now he was back again in that state which every normal woman dreams of.

'Up to then I had not dared to teach him how to put it where I most wanted it, but I became bolder and more shameless and snatched off his nightshirt as I pulled mine over my head. Now there was nothing to prevent me from contemplating his charms in their entirety. I covered them with my hot hands and lips, while he gratefully returned the favour. When his boyish prick was as hard as it ever was going to be,

I made him get on top of me and guided the member to its proper home.

'What an apt pupil he was! Although I was tight, he was not big. Energetically, we shoved ourselves against each other. Now straddling him, I finally succeeded in getting all of it into me with the ineffable satisfaction of realizing that I was going to get what I had so passionately desired for so long. With shudders that ran through both of us, we simultaneously and reciprocally rid ourselves of our not exactly intact virginities.

'Dear heaven! What sensuality we enjoyed! Vernol was almost out of his senses with ecstasy. We experienced that unadulterated felicity which comes only once in a lifetime and which cannot be described in mere words. Our bliss was at its peak. He was the first to savour that glorious excess when he discharged. As he gushed into me, his arms which had held me as if in a vice suddenly became limp.

'Quickening my tempo, I reached the goal instants after, and as I collapsed like a punctured balloon, he knew that I was in the same state of wonderment as he. Glued to each other, we tasted to the dregs that magnificent annihilation which is no less exhilarating than the transports that caused it. Being the first to recover from our swoons, I found that I had immediate need of his hand and finger again.

'Every morning we indulged in this most delightful of all diversions, either in his bed or mine, and during the rest of the day, anyplace where we felt ourselves secure from prying eyes. At night, when we could not be together, I resurrected by myself the day's pleasures while he did the same in his chamber. I knew that because he told me himself. Every morning we exchanged confidences during the realization of our nocturnal illusions.

'Impressed from the very first by all that I had taught him, he urged me to tell him where and how I had acquired my knowledge. At first deeming it imprudent to say anything about my stay with my cousin, I skirted the question with vague generalities, but as our intimacy deepened and my confidence in him grew, I told him the whole story.'

When Rose finished her tale, which she had told me before in more vivid detail, especially about Vernol, I took the floor.

'Dear father, you don't know what else Rose confided in me. She didn't tell you everything.

' "My dearest Laura," she said to me, "Vernol is head over heels in love with you. I saw it right away, and he even admitted it to me. Now, I am not jealous at all, for I love both of you tenderly. You are lovely and he is charming, and nothing would give me greater pleasure than to see you in his arms. Yes, my dear, I would even put you there myself, for his happiness means all the world to me." Don't you think she is slightly out of her mind, Papa?'

'Not very,' my father replied after some thought. 'As a matter of fact, I really am not surprised at all.'

It was easy to see that Rose adored pleasure with a fury. When we told her that, she readily agreed. The tableaux that she had summoned up from the past animated her as they did us. The effect on my father produced an eloquence which Rose immediately seized upon. To show us the delight she found in the beloved object, she slid it into her sanctuary with a prolonged sigh.

After she had reached her climax seconds before my father, she resumed her reflections.

'If you feel that you cannot confide in me after what I have told you about my brother, please disabuse yourselves of the notion. Because of our intimacies since yesterday, I feel free to tell you everything that is in my mind and heart.'

'Come, Papa, and sit next to your daughter,' I interrupted. 'I'll take Rose's place and prove to you that I am every bit her equal. But put that thing in her so that she can experience at the same time the joys you have given me.'

'Well, Rose, you are going to play a new role,' he declared as he rose to fetch the dildo, which he then fastened to her waist.

Rose was ecstatic at the intrument, the likes of which she had never seen before. Making me mount her, Papa guided it into my cunt while telling her to bestir herself like a man and titillate me at the same time. Also, he instructed her how to discharge it when she felt that I was on the verge. Then he got on me in turn and introduced my old playmate into the rear aperture.

As Rose wiggled most lasciviously, she held my breasts as I fondled hers, and when she sucked my tongue, I thought I was dying. Just as I was about to lose consciousness, she released the dildo's contents. My cunt was inundated. At the same time, the fuck that my father spurted into my rear lifted me to new raptures. Rose was not left out of the general bliss, for the rubbing of the dildo against her clitoris had produced an orgasm. I finally succumbed completely, slain by sheer bliss.

My father soon came to, and when I was revived, we all three got out of bed since it was almost noon.

When we were back on our feet and in our clothes, Rose could hardly wait to examine more closely the marvellous strange contraption. After explaining that it was an exact replica, if slightly oversize, of the male organ, I pointed out its features, chiefly the mechanism which jetted hot water or milk so cleverly that the recipient could not distinguish it from real semen.

When I was through, Rose promptly tucked up her skirt and tried to introduce it into her cunt. Her awkward attempts were so comical that I could not help but laugh. My peals were so loud that my father came back into the room to learn what was up. When he saw Rose fumbling with the instrument, he shared my amusement.

'Leave it alone, Rose, because it is not functioning for the time being,' he advised her. 'Besides, we have better things to do.'

When she desisted and began rearranging her dress, he took me by the hand and led me out of the room.

'Laura,' he earnestly began, 'Rose will be the victim of her own passion and fiery temperament. There is no holding her back. Already she is abandoning herself to pleasure with a fury that I have never before seen in a woman. You can bet your last franc that she will pay a heavy penalty for her excesses. The same goes for that poor Vernol whom she has started down the same path. But I wish to take advantage of it in order to carry out some plans that I have in my head.'

Leaving me, he went to find her in my room. Naturally, I put my ear to the door.

'Rose, what you said about your brother's feelings for my Laura is evidence of the deep friendship you two girls have for each other. But can we count on Vernol's discretion as we can on yours? It is absolutely necessary to be sure of this, as you can well imagine.'

'I don't think you need have any worry on that score,' she assured him. 'What could he gain by blabbing except expulsion from our society, which would be unthinkable in view of his sentiments for your daughter. I'll vouch for Vernol, and I beseech you to let him join in our fun. If he were prevented from pouring out his heart to Laura, he would die of grief.'

'All right,' my father consented. 'It seems that everybody is in league against me. For the time being, however, I don't want him to have the slightest inkling of our activities, and I demand your promise that you will not breathe a word. If he knew, he would consider me well compensated, but I insist on his paying me himself for the sacrifice I am making for him. Just forewarn him that he can expect anything and that he will have to consent to anything we demand of him.'

'I'll answer for him as I would for myself,' Rose warmly replied, 'and you can be sure that he won't learn a thing from me without your consent.'

'One thing more,' my father continued. 'I want both of you to know that Laura is my daughter in name only. She is not my flesh and blood, but she is no less dear to me for all of that. Nobody but you and your brother must know of this.' My father's voice was stern as he gave that warning. 'Now, go to your mother with Laura and tell her that we are going to spend the day in the country tomorrow. With her permission, we would like to take you and your brother with us. And promise me that you and Laura will behave yourselves until the time when we can give free reign to our fantasies.'

When the colloquy, of which I did not miss a word, was over, Rose came to get me. We hurried to her mother who readily granted my father's request. Leaving my friend to her own resources, I spent the rest of the day with a cousin who lived nearby. In the meantime, my father was supervising the arrangements for the next day's project.

At night, when I was nestled in his arms, I asssumed he was going to tell me about his talk with Rose and the excursion the following day, but he fell asleep without saying a word. Disappointed and frustrated, I soon followed his example.

Early the next afternoon, there stopped before our gate a coach which carried us to a charming villa at some distance from the city. Since I had never seen it before, I suspected that it belonged to one of his friends who had placed it at his disposal. Vernol had done his best to improve on his native attractions, and Rose and I were wearing fetching summer dresses in the latest style. Since Rose had explained certain matters to him, he was more at ease and self-assured. When we finally arrived about four, the weather was still perfect.

We made several turns in the gardens whose natural beauty was not crushed by the artificiality so in style today. From among the shrubbery and the flower beds, we gazed at the horizon whose iridescence seemed to be in accord with our mood. After the promenade, we entered the house and went through the suites of rooms. In the main salon where my father led us a delicious repast was being readied for us. As we consumed the appetizing dishes, my father was not sparing with the superb wines he poured.

Whether it was the juice of the grape or some other stimulant, I do not know, but we soon felt its effects. Our heads were whirling as we pelted each other with the petals from the flowers of our garlands. When father noticed the state we were in, he dismissed all the servants with orders not to return until they were summoned. Now we were by ourselves.

We were almost staggering as he led us to an apartment which we had missed on our tour, for it was situated in the most remote part of the villa. From there he ushered us into an intimate salon illuminated on all sides by candles in holders at a height at which they could be easily extinguished by hand. Below them and all around the room ran mirrors with drapes hung in festoons. Scattered around the chamber were big easy-chairs, very low and almost without backs, which were covered with large soft cushions.

On the walls hung various paintings, but what paintings they were! Heavens! In his wildest flights of fancy, Aretino himself could not have conjured up such images. Also, there were statues of figures in highly suggestive positions. In an elaborately decorated niche was to be seen a piece of furniture which sensuousness and voluptuousness had converted into their throne. The surroundings and the wine now dispelled the last of our inhibitions. We were seized by a sort of delirium, with Bacchus and Madness leading the frenzied dance.

Rose, inspired by her favourite deity, Venus, gave the pitch and commenced the hymn of pleasure by flinging herself at my father's neck, embracing Vernol, and hotly kissing me with an invitation to follow her example. Snatching the scarf that covered my bosom, she threw it to her brother and then sailed hers to my father. She made the men kiss her rosepointed globes and then transferred their lips to my welcoming hemispheres.

These frolics reflected infinitely in the mirrors around us aroused us to dizzying heights of lubricity. Our cheeks were flushed, our lips parched and burning, our eyes glittering, and our hearts pounding madly. Vernol, whose clothes were already in disarray, appeared to me as beautiful as the dawn with his glowing complexion and dancing eyes. I regarded him with the adoration of a god, all of whose attractions were concentrated into a single object in the centre of his body, it being the object of all my desires. Although he was unaware of what condition it was in, my father perceived its gradual growth.

In trying to force me down on one of the settees, Rose called for her brother to help her. By parting and lifting my robe, she enabled him to see that for which he was pining. I tried to get revenge by reversing her on her back in turn, but she beat me to it. She threw herself down on it, and kicking her legs up in the air, she unashamedly displayed all the gifts nature had endowed her with – her fetching cunt, her rounded bottom, her flat belly and her satiny thighs – all were visible to the eye.

Immediately, the three of us were at her side to lavish on her the caresses she made clear she so ardently desired. Scarcely had we placed our hands on her buttocks than, with two or three spasms and a roll of the eyes, the fountain of pleasure gushed. Rose and I soon perceived that my father and Vernol had erections straining at their bonds. With an abrupt movement, Rose was at my father's side.

'Dear Papa, I threw you my scarf. That means you will be my husband, and I shall be your wife. Give me your hand!' she imperiously commanded.

'Willingly, my dear Rose,' my father answered, 'but the ceremony only takes place at the end.'

'That is all right with me,' she assented. 'But Vernol caught Laurette's. We have to bring them together, don't you think?'

'Just as you wish.'

She hurriedly took our hands which she clasped in each other's. When she made us kiss, our mouths obediently obeyed the order. Placing her hand on my bare bosom, she pronounced us man and wife. If our senses were overheated, Rose was on fire.

'How refreshing it would be to have a bath. Right now,' she exclaimed. 'I feel as if I were burning up.'

My father rose to pull a cord in the alcove. When he did so, the throne slid back, revealing a pool with three taps that sprayed cool, warm, or hot water.

'Isn't this marvellous?' Rose chortled gleefully. 'It's an enchanted palace. I'm going to be a naiad, but not all by myself.'

In a flash, she appeared wearing the usual costume of water fairies, namely, nothing at all. Grabbing hold of me, she urged my father and Vernol to aid her in stripping me to a similar state. Before I could utter a word, I was down to the buff. When Rose made a signal, Vernol pranced out like a satyr. That left only my father, whom Rose and I were busily disgarbing.

My furtive eyes were already scrutinizing Vernol. What a handsome and seductive figure he cut! He bloomed with the freshness of youth, and in the middle of all the alabaster whiteness of his skin, skin that a young girl would have envied, proudly rose the distinguishing mark of a man.

Consumed by devouring flames, we were like those furnaces which sizzle when water is thrown on them and then only burn hotter. Two pointed lances were aimed at Rose and myself, but the prospect of combat did not daunt us. Our bodies prey to the frisky hands and lascivious lips of the Tritons, Rose and I happily returned their advances instead of rebuffing them and toyed with their arrows as they manipulated our quivers. At that moment, my father was prudent enough to shove a sponge into mine when I was least expecting it.

Vernol wanted to enter the lists against me, but with the adroitness so natural to women and so calculated to stimulate desire, I nimbly stepped aside and sprang out of the tub. When Rose followed me, the men were soon out, too. The effect that the dip had on them was visible from the condition of their crests. Their temporary humiliation gave us a chance to dry ourselves and don diaphanous robes which concealed nothing from their larcenous eyes. Then we all stretched out languorously on the easy-chairs. Hardly had we settled ourselves than my father, giving a jerk on another cord, had lowered before us a table heaped with delicacies and wines like those that had intoxicated us shortly before. All was there to augment the ardour which was rising again in us.

Vernol was so impatient that he was twitching as he reclined on his chair. What surprised me was Rose's seemingly unabated exuberance. As for myself, for whom voluptuousness was a more refined enjoyment, I preferred to wait and watch before attaining the goal. The anticipation gave me almost as great pleasure as the realization. My father was also firmly of the opinion that the postponement of satisfaction gave it more spice when it was finally tasted.

Consequently, Vernol and Rose had to chafe under the yoke of unrequited desire. It was easier for Rose who, under our touches and fondling, had reached bliss three times already, according to her own admission. She called the collation a wedding banquet, even though no maidenhead presided over it. But what did it matter? Voluptuousness held sway, and we were content under her rule. Crowned by the sylvan deity, she was to be seen in the centre of the table with the sceptre in her hand. In the four corners of the alcove were entwined pairs in the most lascivious positions. Flitting among them were old envious satyrs making their pitiful offerings which the nymphs scornfully refused, for here all was merriment and animation.

The impetuous Rose, with a bottle and a glass in her hand and robe open to reveal her seductive conniceties, sent flames racing through our veins. What she poured us became a torrent of fire. Now I was boiling inside, and our partners were in the same state of lust, judging from their virilities.

No longer able to restrain herself, Rose lifted her

glass and cried out: 'Vernol, take your bride?' Then, throwing herself into my father's arm, she again shouted: 'And here I have my husband!'

She had firm possession of his prick, which she was getting ready to insert into its proper slot, and Vernol had one arm around my waist and the hand of the other on my cunt, when my father put a stop to the proceedings.

'Just a moment, children!' he announced. 'There is a condition I am laying down for my consent to continue, and it is only right that it be met. If Vernol is to penetrate Laura, I insist on following the example of that courtier who, after coupling his wife with a young page she was sleeping with, did in the lad's rear what the latter was doing in the lady's front. Therefore, if Vernol wants to fuck Laura, I demand that his bottom be at my disposition.'

So, I thought, Vernol's charms had attracted my father as much they had me. At first, I felt a twinge of jealousy, but then I reflected that I would be freer with Vernol if my father was not watching me, and I did my best to enhance the pleasure of their game.

Roughly ripping off Vernol's robe, I made my father an offering of his rump, the rounded cheeks of which I spread wide. Oblivious to my actions, the boy was preparing to plunge his prick into my chasm.

'No, no, Vernol,' I chided him as I would a naughty child. 'Don't deceive yourself into thinking that you can put it into me without fulfilling that stipulation my father made.'

'Oh, Laura!' he panted. 'You can put any obstacle in my path and I shall overcome it. I have been in hell

107

for an eternity, and there isn't anything I wouldn't do to have you and expire in your arms.'

'We can't leave Rose out of our little party,' my father said, interrupting Vernol's impassioned declaration.

The table was whisked away, and a thick soft mat covered the flooring over the pool. Now the alcove was a true sanctuary of lust. In a flash, we relieved ourselves of all that we had not entered the world with. Adorned only with what nature had seen fit to give us, we made obeisances at the altar to the divinity we all worshipped from the bottom of our hearts.

On all sides the mirrors reflected endlessly our various charms. When Vernol cast admiring glances on mine, he swept me into his arms and covered me with kisses and caresses, while his prick, which I was firmly clutching, stood as firm as a rock. My father was massaging his buttocks with one hand, while with the other, he was busy with Rose's breasts or slit. She, in turn, was all over us.

Finally yielding to his amorous frenzy, Vernol turned me on my back, widened the space between my thighs, kissed my Venus mount and valley, darted his tongue into it, sucked my clitoris, mounted me, and finally jabbed his prick into me up to the hilt.

In the meantime, my father had taken his position behind him. Rose, on her knees and supporting herself on her elbows, and with her fur-fringed cavern before my face, spread still wider her brother's rear cheeks, noistened the entry with her tongue, and guided my father's prick along the path she had cleared. While they were bucking up and down in rhythm, she impartially was tickling the testicles of each. In her cunt I

108

had my finger, which I energetically kept pushing in and out. Again, it was she who first came to bliss, but Vernol was not far behind. When my father noticed his victim's sudden stiffening and relaxation, he redoubled his efforts which added greatly to my pleasures. Keeping time with his quickened tempo, I plunged down the dizzy descent of ecstasy along with him, and we landed at the bottom side by side. The three of us were now, one could say, a single unit which Rose was bathing with her wet lips.

When it was over, we paused to catch our breath. Still breathing heavily, Vernol asserted that he had never experienced such raptures in his life.

'What you have received you should give,' my father drily remarked. 'Come, Laura, let's see what he can do. Although he is not so well equipped as I, I am quite sure that you will not be dissatisfied with him. While he and I taste of your delights. Rose will repeat her performance, but this time she will stimulate your clitoris with her hand from behind.'

Jumping on my sire, I feverishly caressed his body as Rose introduced his prick into my cunt. After this task was performed, she parted the cheeks of my derriere and took her brother's virility into her mouth. When the organ was sufficiently hardened and moistened, she led it to its goal. She titillated me as she massaged her brother's buttocks. At the same time, my father, his finger in her slit, was nearly driving her out of her mind with lust.

When the sublime presence was announcing himself, we all flew after it and caught it. Oh, how magnificent and superb he was! We all spurted, drenching ourselves with the fluid that began dribbling down the sides of our bodies. I was in such a rapture that I could barely contain myself. After floundering around like a drowning swimmer, I felt come over me a calm, that was no less voluptuous than the climax itself. The contraction of my muscles and the friction of all the sensitive, delicate parts where sensuousness reigns were almost too much.

There was no question but that we had to get some rest. We were able to persuade our male partners to put back on their robes, if only for the time being, but that did little to soothe our taut nerves. Our eyes, hands, mouths, and tongues all bespoke desire, and our conversation concerned nothing else. Rose's and my breasts, buttocks and cunts were massaged and reverently kissed, tokens of affection which we returned on their pricks, nipples and testicles. There was no mistaking the reaction – the vanquished members had risen proudly to renew the struggle with our distended clitorises.

Now Rose had a role with more meat than those she had played before. After I had made her lie down with her knees raised, my father rested himself along side of her, and passing his thighs under her legs, he aimed his prick at the target.

Joining the fray, I got on top of her with her head between my knees and those of Vernol, who was doing it to me in the fashion of a dog. I put my father's instrument into her slippery slit where it went in and out like a piston. In turn, he played first with my breasts and then with her opulent pendants. As he was thus engaged, Rose and I amused ourselves by irritating each other's rosy buttons. She could not keep her fascinated eyes off Vernol's prick which was

rising and falling in time with the swaying appendages. It produced such a powerful effect on her that
during the time we were striving for the initial ecstasy,
she had savoured in four times. Four times she
moaned in a dying voice, 'I'm coming! I'm dying!'
She was an inexhaustible fountain. A fifth copious
overflow blended with my father's boiling jet, one that
flooded her.

With their pleasure prodding us, Vernol and I
reached the summit almost simultaneously. This time,
Rose seemed as if she were parting this life. The bliss
she had been chasing had not escaped her eager grasp.
Her cunt was a morass of fuck and no wonder, for
she had three or four orgasms to our one. After
writhing and biting and scratching, she fell into that
prostration in which one feels nothing but the most
delicious fatigue.

When she came to, she could not praise highly
enough the variation and she made up her mind that
she could study it more closely. As soon as we came
to, we changed places. I took her place, with her on
top of me, while she was being fucked by her brother.
Since my head was between their thighs, I was able
to follow at close range all their motions. At the same
time, my father gave free rein to his fancy with me.

When this fourth act was over, we were so broken
that it was imperative to take time out again. After
we unsteadily got to our feet, my father had the table
lowered again and we gulped down the food as if we
were famished. Sleep was also a necessity. As soon as
the table was lifted away, the four of us lay down on
the matting, one on top or beside the other, our arms

and legs interlaced, and each clutching the object of his desires.

After an hour of respose, Rose, awakened by a sultry dream, shook us out of our lethargy. Our gambols commenced anew, but instead of rushing headlong into the maelstrom of sensuousness, we toyed with our urges in order to make them last longer and enhance their intensity. We made advances to pleasure and then pushed it away but, aroused in turn, it pursued us. Only Rose allowed herself to be captured, and she surrendered two or three times before it abandoned her to catch up with us. We were just as helpless before its might. It is not a thing to be trifled with. We finally ended the day with a fifth act, in which Rose played the leading role.

As she was lying on my father who was taking the main highway on her body, Vernol presented himself at the rear gate. I assumed her former position, rendering them the same services I had received. At the same time, my father had his wandering hands all over the hills and dales of my body. Perhaps for the sake of change, Vernol from time to time took different roads. He veered from the one I had started him on to join up with my father on his path. Rose was overjoyed to see them united in such a way, side by side on the same narrow way which barely accommodated the two of them, but at the last moment, he returned to the thoroughfare I had chosen for him. She found this, too, utterly divine. It was not difficult to please Rose.

'Death would be sweet if it came at such a delicious moment!' she cried enthusiastically.

Although we smiled at her flight of fancy, we found

it quite in keeping with her temperament and mentality.

Before dressing, my father made the pool appear again. Without any ado, I immersed myself in its refreshing water. The others promptly followed me. I pulled out the sponge and vigorously washed the hole it had occupied. This second ablution calmed our nerves, and since it was getting late, we made preparations for our departure. The coach appeared at eight, and we were back in the city an hour or so later.

During the ensuing days, Rose kept after me to play similar games with her. I finally yielded, and I have to admit I enjoyed them. But after a while, the sport palled, a fact which my father noted with his sharp eyes. He was not displeased. And I began losing interest in Vernol. My initial infatuation with him merely resulted from the impression made on my eyes and hands. I felt nothing in my heart for him. If you took away his good looks and manners, there was not much left. Finally, it was over and I had few or no regrets.

From then on, I followed only the dictates of my heart which led me back to my father, whom I loved and adored more than ever. I considered him an extraordinary man, unique, and a true philosopher far above the mundane, but at the same time appealing and seductive to a woman's sensitivities. He had the qualities that hold our fair sex in fetters and that can clip the wings of our inborn inconstancy. Thinking men make no protest when they are faced with it, but they are able to put a stop to it. Finally,

I was in reality the sole object of his affection, just as he became to me. These feelings for him, and several incidents, caused me to break off completely my tenuous liaisons.

An adventure during which Rose snapped several lances with too much insolence caused my final alienation from her and Vernol. Added to that was the account of a particularly loathsome adventure they confided to me. Now I was convinced that fastidiousness was not to be found in either of them and that their emotions were ruled only by unbridled lust and passion. Their way of life and thought was not in accord with mine at all.

Since I rarely saw them, they took their pleasures where they found them, and their favourite hunting ground was the public park. One day, as Vernol was taking a stroll on the promenade with his sister, he came across four of his old school comrades, the oldest of whom was about twenty. Joyfully, they recognized each other, embraced, and hurled questions and answers back and forth.

'Where are you coming from? What are you doing? Where are you going? Who is this bewitching creature?'

Rose, of course, did not take their flattery and compliments amiss. Once their curiosities were satisfied, they insisted that Vernol and his sister join their party and go with them to an inn where they had planned a light meal.

At the outset, the young people obeyed social conventions, but the oldest, who was also the craftiest, began to exert his wiles for his underhanded purposes. As they briskly paced to their destination, the polite

114

language turned into double-entendres and off-colour jokes and stories.

Once in their room, Rose flounced on the bed saying that she was hot. As she did so, she revealed her snowy bosom and a well-turned leg. Such praise was rained on her charms that she nearly reeled with delight. After the meal had been consumed and while the wine was being drunk, heads became giddy. Rose tossed off some more champagne with the others following her example. In the general hilarity, the innuendos became more unmistakable and liberties were freely taken and given. Touches became embraces and embraces led to kisses. The fire was lit and soon was to blaze.

The senior, more brazen and experienced than his companions, took Vernol aside and told him what they had planned. At first, he looked stupefied, but then he held his sides with laughter. Curious as usual, Rose insisted on learning what the joke was about. After succumbing to her wiles and pestering, he told her that before they had met her and Vernol, they had agreed among themselves that the one of the quartet with the biggest prick would pay for the wine and the one with the smallest would pay for the rest.

When she heard that, Rose almost choked with merriment. She was so convulsed with laughter that when she fell back on the bed with her legs up in the air she revealed practically everything that a woman should keep concealed.

'Who's going to be judge?' she demanded when she had recovered from her hysteria.

'Why you, of course,' the senior replied as if it were the most natural thing in the world.

Animated by the wine and flattered by the invitation, Rose declared that she was well qualified to take on the judicial chore.

From that moment, all restraint was cast aside and the inhabitants of the room were shameless in their antics. A valiant and battle-scarred warrior, Rose held her own with the best of them and was prepared and ready for more interesting assaults than verbal ones. Eager to bring matters to a head as quickly as possible, she beckoned Vernol to her, and wrapping an arm around his neck, she forced his head down to kiss the breasts she had flipped out of her bodice. Then sliding her other hand down to his trousers, she undid the buttons and yanked out his straining prick.

In revenge, he slipped his hand up under her skirts where he quickly won possession of her cunt that was already beginning to dribble. When she kicked up a knee, her centre of pleasure was visible in all its glory to the others. The sight so awed the group that they eagerly gathered around her. One took hold of a posterior cheek, another a part of the thigh, still another one of her snowy globes. Each now had a part of her. As she made Vernol rise, she asked if any of them could produce its equal. At that, each immediately had a competitor in his hand. Now before her eyes was the dazzling spectacle of five proudly standing pricks, arrogant and menacing, which dared her to combat, even though they knew they were sure to lose.

Sitting up for a better view of the jousting site, she gave the quintet's pride and joy a quick but careful scrutiny.

'I could come to a decision right now,' Rose

asserted, 'but as a judge, I want to take every possible precaution. I'll have to use some sort of measure, even my own if necessary, so I won't be accused of making a biased judgment. Let's begin.'

Using her boot-lace as a tape, she conscientiously took the measurements of each, both in length and diameter, and with the same care weighed their appendages in her hand. Manipulating all these instruments of pleasure affected her so deeply that she fell on her back again. The two or three convulsive wiggles of her derriere were evidence that she was discharging.

It was as if they had heared the starting signals of a race, the way they rushed to mount her.

'Before we proceed,' she said, stopping them by imperiously raising her hand, 'I wish to announce my findings. I hereby order the senior to foot the bill for the wine. If my brother had been a party to your pact, he would have been obligated for the remainder of the bill, but since he wasn't, I bestow that honour on number two.'

Seeing the latter's crestfallen expression, she comforted him by saying that it would grow with his years and that he would be the first to have her, which would be very soon, since all those pricks and testicles had set her aflame.

Stretching herself flat on her back, she beckoned to the lad, who needed no second invitation. He leaped on her and in a flash, his dart was in the ring she proffered him. Vernol followed him in turn, and then came the three others according to the gradations she had measured. The overjoyed Rose was wallowing in fuck and bliss. Spurting almost incessantly, she scarcely had time to catch her breath, for no sooner had one left the lists than another took his place.

There finally came the moment when she could not any more, and the entr'acte was spent in drinking, laughing and cuddling. She was willing prey to the impassioned kisses and foraging hands of her five gallants. Since they did not tolerate a stitch of clothing on her, she was promptly in the state of the goddesses during the Judgment of Paris.

The ravishing sight revived their forces and desires to a fury. Wistfully, she wished she had five cunts so she could have enjoyed them all simultaneously, but she had to be satisfied with having them in twos.

Always impatient for variety, she made the champion lie on the bed with his head at the foot, and then climbed onto him so that her breasts dangled directly above his mouth. The least favoured youngster got on her between her thighs. When they were in position, they each took the indicated road. Now squeezed in a tight vice, she clutched the envious members of the other two, while she took Vernol's bauble between her lips, alternatively sucking and tickling it with her tongue.

Although sperm was running down all over her body, she remained unconquered after twenty-five engagements during which time she irrigated the field of battle twenty-nine times. She was worn out, but deliciously so.

I saw her the following day. At first, I thought she was on the point of death with her languid eyes and listless body. Surprised at finding her in such a sad state, I questioned her and kept at it until she and Vernol told me all about the orgy.

I did not bother to give them any advice, for I knew how useless it would be. I did not even deign to scold them. The reader is undoubtedly aware that they resumed their former activities as promptly as they could. That was the last time I saw them, but I heard about their ends.

Unable to stop herself in her mad drive for pleasure. Rose finally succumbed to it. When she stopped menstruating, she had an abortion, which took a terrible toll on her. She suffered from agonizing fits of dizziness and her sight began to fail. She more resembled a walking wraith than a human being. The cheerful spirited young woman had vanished. Finally, the lingering illness brought her to the grave.

Vernol, who was his sister's faithful companion in all her escapades, shortly after came down with a virulent fever which nearly carried him off, and no sooner had he recovered than he contracted the pox which permanently disfigured his handsome features. It was not long before he was laid to rest at Rose's side.

My father had foreseen that something like this would happen, and afterwards, we often discussed it. Better than ever, I knew the good care he had given me, and my gratitude knew no bounds at having escaped such a tragic fate. Our relationship gradually deepened, but the feelings we had for each other were more tender, more sensuous and refined than passionate. Many nights we spent together in bed with no sensation other than the quiet satisfaction of knowing that the other was there.

One evening, I suddenly remembered all my past indiscretions, which I now considered acts of infidelity, and I burst into tears. Immediately he was at my side, comforting me and asking what was wrong.

'How can you have any esteem for me after the way I treated you?' I sobbed. 'I'm nothing but a debauchee who was unfaithful to you.'

'Have you taken leave of your senses, my child!' he asked in astonishment. 'What does it matter if a woman has lain in the arms of another lover, if her heart and mind remain true? Is the worth of a woman to be judged by how often she has been used? And wasn't I then unfaithful to you with my dalliances with Lucette, Rose, and even Vernol? And yet you know that there is nobody whom I love as much as I do you. So no more much nonsense.'

I was reassured and comforted.

Then tragedy struck. Its first heartless blow had been the death of dear Lucette, the news of which saddened us, my father even more than myself. Although he was his usual kind self always, I noticed a change in him afterwards. Many times I caught a sombre expression on his face.

I was twenty when my father, the most lovable man who ever walked the face of the earth, for whom I would have cheerfully laid down my life, caught pneumonia, and all the arts of medicine were unable to save him. Day and night I was by his bed which I wet with my tears as he feebly ran his hand through my hair. The end came and his last sigh was breathed on my lips.

What a loss! I was more devoted to him than if he had really been my father. He had introduced me to the Count de Norval, to whose amorous activities I owed the light of the day, and whom I regarded with no emotion other than a slight curiosity.

My grief was such that I nearly went out of my mind. I could not even find surcease in sleep since it never came. Soon I, too, came down with a fever which turned into a serious illness. I wanted to die, but my hour had not yet come, for my youth saved me against my will.

When I regained my health, I determined to bury myself alive. Having lost everything that counted, I loathed life. I entered a convent.

If it had not been for the solicitude of Eugenie, I am sure I would have perished behind those forbidding walls. Without knowing the cause of my sorrow, she was still able to touch the bottom of my heart. Never was she too busy to come and dry my tears and dissipate my apathy. Her tenderness and sympathy lent weight to her consolatory words, but the night toppled all that she had built during the day. That she quickly recognized, and she obtained permission to share my bed. I was surprised at the treasures concealed beneath her wimple and robe. When she found that my spirits had picked up some, she urged me to tell her the whole mournful story.

After her kindness, I could not rebuff her and I began recounting my life piecemeal. I knew that I needed a friend, but I despaired over finding one again. It was at such moments that I realized what I had lost in Lucette. And I never dreamed that I would find a replacement in Eugenie. As our intimacy deepened, I repaid her confidences with mine, and in her arms I found the balm for my pain.

Never shall I forget a certain night when she spoke to me even more tenderly than was her wont.

'Dearest Laura,' she said, squeezing me to her, 'I know that you're suffering, but if I can dull the edge of your grief by confiding in you what I am undergoing and have undergone, nothing would make me happier. Listen, my dear, I love you. I love you with all my heart, even though a cruel fate has decreed that I have to wear a religious habit.

'Hypocritical nuns surrounded my innocent childhood with walls and bars and sucked me into their infernal dungeons. Ignorance and prejudice are my tormentors and desire my executioner. During the night, I am unable to shut my eyes because of the tears that fill them. By day, I am disgusted or bored with all I see and hear. Compare yourself to me. At least, you can leave here whenever you wish to give a lover the charms that I have glimpsed and am now touching.'

The soft hand that she placed on my breast sent a thrill running up and down my spine.

'He has come back to me!' I cried deliriously. 'I lost him to death, but now he has been returned to me.'

As I tightly pressed her to me, it was my father whom I was embracing. Such was the illusion she had produced in me. But as I ran my hand over her body, there was one thing lacking that snapped me back to reality. But her other delicacies that I tasted with my tongue compensated for the lack. Her bosom, her figure, her derriere, her skin and her mound were incomparable.

'What a delight it would be for you if only a lover

122

could hold you in his arms as I am now,' I ecstatically exclaimed. 'You once said you wanted to know about these forbidden pleasures, and if the raptures were as great as they were claimed to be. Now I shall give you some idea, that is, if you wish.'

Her curiosity and desire, both at white heat, led her to accept my invitation. For my part, the wish to console her and tear away the veil of ignorance made me forget temporarily my own woes. She proved to be an apt and conscientious pupil.

Spreading apart her legs, I grazed with my fingers the lips of her narrow cunt whose roses were just starting to bloom. I did not dare insert a digit, for the initial pain would hardly be a suitable introduction to enjoyment. Soon, however, I won the throne of voluptuousness with its fetching clitoris that I slightly irritated. She was thrown into a spasm of ecstasy from which she had the greatest difficulty in recovering.

'Dearest Laura,' she murmured weakly, 'I never dreamt that there was anything like this in the world.'

She in turn awkwardly made me her lover and my body was covered with impassioned kisses and feverish hands as she tried to return the raptures I had given her. But I was still too sad at heart to be receptive, and I stopped her hand. Instead, I took her back in my arms and, renewing my tokens of affection, I put her on the first step towards bliss.

'This is so wonderful,' she sighed. 'Do anything you wish to me, but never stop.'

When my hand slipped back to her darling little cunt and I started to probe it, she squirmed at the exquisite pain.

'It is I, dear friend,' I whispered into her ear, 'it is

I, happiest of mortals, who plucked your maidenhead, that rarest and most sought after of blossoms.'

Now that she had taken the first sip of sensuousness, I no longer hesitated to open my heart to her completely and I recounted to her all the adventures set down on these pages. If I was able to free her from the yoke of ignorance, it was no problem to rid her of the last vestiges of prejudice. After telling her of my own experiences, the fear of pregnancy no longer troubled her.

'Everything you tell me and do to me runs counter to what the nuns have taught,' she panted.

Her trust in me, my counsel, and my assistance brushed away the last crumbling obstacles on the road of sensuality. The peace of mind she enjoys today was due entirely to my efforts, and her lover owes his victory to me. Yes, my friendship served them both well.

Before completing her education, I wanted to meet the Monsieur Valsay so dear to her heart, make sure of his character, and ascertain if he was worthy of her love, her confidence and her favours.

When I met Valsay, I liked what I saw and heard. I felt no qualms about letting him have Eugenie, rouse and satisfy her yearnings, enlighten her and banish her fears.

Yet, had it not been for me, Eugenie would never have completely overcome her timidity. When he pressed her with the most heartbreaking importunities to make him happy, and she refused him, even though she desperately wanted him, I took his side. At the mment when her ardour was becoming almost too much for her I decided it was time for me to intervene, only too happy with the thought that I was contributing to their felicity.

Now I am going to remove the last of the hindrances,' I informed them. 'Valsay, you will be a pure ingrate, one unworthy of the inestimable prize I am about to bestow on you, if my conduct toward this end lowers me in your esteem.'

Earnestly, he assured me that that would never happen.

In spite of Eugenie's protests, I closed the door of the reception room and then almost dragged her to the grille against which Valsay was pressing his face. I did not forget to tear off her veil. There he eagerly grasped for her saucy breasts, kissed her lips, and sucked the tip of the tongue she stuck out in spite of herself.

His overpowering desire gave him courage to insert his hand up inside her skirt to reach and possess the *mons Veneris*. I pushed her still closer to him, kissing her for reassurance at the same time. Finally, he was able to raise the robe up to her waist and contemplate that delightful little cunt with all its ornaments of untouched youth.

His hands wandering over her yielding body were like tinder on her inner bonfire. Vainly he cursed and kicked the implacable grille that separated us and opposed his desire. My heart was almost breaking at the touching sight.

'What?' I taunted him scornfully, although I did not mean it. 'Are you so lacking in resourcefulness that these bars are going to be an insuperable barrier to what you say you so ardently want? True love always finds a way. But I also love Eugenie, and I shall prove it, for there is nothing more I want than to make the two of you happy.'

The squares formed by the iron bars were larger further up. First, I firmly tucked up the hem of the black religious garb which contrasted so dazzlingly with the alabaster of her firmly rounded rump, which he massaged, kissed, and paid the homage due to it. Then I got down on all fours and made her stand on my back so that the little slit was framed like a picture by the bars of the upper square. Valsay, unable to withhold a gasp of admiration, pulled up a chair on which he stood to be at the same level as she. Almost yanking out the organ in which all his desire was concentrated, he thrust it into her hollow as I slipped my hand through her thighs to assist him. Slowly but surely, that sensation we term passion began to exert its irresistible pressure on her. She was swaying back and forth on my back, when I felt her stiffen. A few hot drops of liquid dropped down on my skin.

Just before he was to emulate her, he discreetly withdrew and spattered my back like a hailstorm. Then I left the happy couple to their own devices.

When Eugenie saw the jewel I had so often described and praised, she took it almost gingerly in her hand and fondled it, but it was apparent that she still did not know quite what to do with it. Bashful about admitting her ignorance, she made muffled laments which quickly brought me back to her side, and when I was there, she beseeched me not to leave her. Generously, I offered to lend whatever further assistance was required. Now she was as gleeful as a child with a new toy.

It was then that I reminded her of the beneficial

sponge, about which I had told her. When she returned with the primitive contraceptive, I had a chair ready for her to supplant my back. Touched by my thoughtfulness, she insisted that I stay to witness the consummation.

With her hand, she exposed to me the divinity between Valsay's legs. Then she revealed to him my breasts, which, to my surprise, I found had retained all their curvaceous charm, and everything else that a decent woman keeps concealed. She even permitted him to touch them. If they only knew what a jerk of emotion they aroused in me.

When I whispered to her how I felt, the little traitoress shamelessly blurted out my secret to him. She was insistent that I, too, enjoy the favours of her lover. She wanted me also to have the most precious thing she owned. When she tried to make me take her place on the chair, I resisted in spite of her pleas and urgings. The blood in my veins had turned to lava, but I still held fast.

'No, Eugenie,' I said firmly. 'I shall never consent to something like that, no matter what you say. After all I suffered, I made up my mind to renounce any intimate relationships with men, and I shall not be shaken from this resolution. In spite of the sensations you have awakened in me. I am happy and content just to lie and rest in your arms at night when you quench the flames that you lit during the day.'

With that, I hurried away to let her lose her virginity without me.

A fate jealous of my contentment decided to destroy it. Eugenie and I were separated when urgent matters concerning my inheritance forced me to leave the convent sooner than I had intended.

As I had promised, I wrote her almost daily during my absence. Even through letters, we remained as close as we ever had been. She knew the attraction she held for me just as I knew how she cherished me.

As I conclude this account, I sigh for the warmth of her arms around me and her lips on mine. Inwardly, I send her a thousand kisses which I hope soon to be able to give her personally. When we meet, I shall have for her a little jewel similar to Valsay's but not so dangerous, but one which will fill a certain gap. Since Valsay has been recalled to his regiment and will be gone for some time, the perilous liaison will fade away and I shall soon be at her side to dry her tears.

Wait for me, my dearest.

# MORE EROTIC CLASSICS FROM CARROLL & GRAF

☐ Anonymous/ALTAR OF VENUS $3.95
☐ Anonymous/AUTOBIOGRAPHY OF A
FLEA $3.95
☐ Anonymous/THE CELEBRATED MISTRESS $3.95
☐ Anonymous/CONFESSIONS OF AN ENGLISH
MAID $3.95
☐ Anonymous/CONFESSIONS OF EVELINE $3.95
☐ Anonymous/COURT OF VENUS $3.95
☐ Anonymous/DANGEROUS AFFAIRS $3.95
☐ Anonymous/THE DIARY OF MATA HARI $3.95
☐ Anonymous/DOLLY MORTON $3.95
☐ Anonymous/THE EDUCATION OF A
MAIDEN $3.95
☐ Anonymous/THE EROTIC READER $3.95
☐ Anonymous/THE EROTIC READER II $3.95
☐ Anonymous/THE EROTIC READER III $4.50
☐ Anonymous/FANNY HILL'S DAUGHTER $3.95
☐ Anonymous/FLORENTINE AND JULIA $3.95
☐ Anonymous/A LADY OF QUALITY $3.95
☐ Anonymous/LENA'S STORY $3.95
☐ Anonymous/THE LIBERTINES $4.50
☐ Anonymous/LOVE PAGODA $3.95
☐ Anonymous/THE LUSTFUL TURK $3.95
☐ Anonymous/MADELEINE $3.95
☐ Anonymous/A MAID'S JOURNEY $3.95
☐ Anonymous/MAID'S NIGHT IN $3.95
☐ Anonymous/THE OYSTER $3.95
☐ Anonymous/THE OYSTER II $3.95
☐ Anonymous/THE OYSTER III $4.50
☐ Anonymous/PARISIAN NIGHTS $4.50
☐ Anonymous/PLEASURES AND FOLLIES $3.95
☐ Anonymous/PLEASURE'S MISTRESS $3.95
☐ Anonymous/PRIMA DONNA $3.95
☐ Anonymous/ROSA FIELDING: VICTIM OF
LUST $3.95
☐ Anonymous/SATANIC VENUS $4.50
☐ Anonymous/SECRET LIVES $3.95
☐ Anonymous/THREE TIMES A WOMAN $3.95

| | |
|---|---|
| ☐ Anonymous/VENUS DISPOSES | $3.95 |
| ☐ Anonymous/VENUS IN PARIS | $3.95 |
| ☐ Anonymous/VENUS UNBOUND | $3.95 |
| ☐ Anonymous/VENUS UNMASKED | $3.95 |
| ☐ Anonymous/VICTORIAN FANCIES | $3.95 |
| ☐ Anonymous/THE WANTONS | $3.95 |
| ☐ Anonymous/A WOMAN OF PLEASURE | $3.95 |
| ☐ Anonymous/WHITE THIGHS | $4.50 |
| ☐ Perez, Faustino/LA LOLITA | $3.95 |
| ☐ van Heller, Marcus/ADAM & EVE | $3.95 |
| ☐ van Heller, Marcus/THE FRENCH WAY | $3.95 |
| ☐ van Heller, Marcus/THE HOUSE OF BORGIA | $3.95 |
| ☐ van Heller, Marcus/THE LOINS OF AMON | $3.95 |
| ☐ van Heller, Marcus/ROMAN ORGY | $3.95 |
| ☐ van Heller, Marcus/VENUS IN LACE | $3.95 |
| ☐ Villefranche, Anne-Marie/FOLIES D'AMOUR | $3.95 |
|     Cloth | $14.95 |
| ☐ Villefranche, Anne-Marie/JOIE D'AMOUR | $3.95 |
|     Cloth | $13.95 |
| ☐ Villefranche, Anne-Marie/ MYSTERE D'AMOUR | $3.95 |
| ☐ Villefranche, Anne-Marie/PLAISIR D'AMOUR | $3.95 |
|     Cloth | $12.95 |
| ☐ Von Falkensee, Margarete/BLUE ANGEL NIGHTS | $3.95 |
| ☐ Von Falkensee, Margarete/BLUE ANGEL SECRETS | $4.50 |